MURDER AT THE JOSHUA TREE

From Our Outfit to yours
All The Best

Ron McCoy

MURDER
AT THE JOSHUA TREE

A Desert Mystery

RON McCOY

Published by **Many Seasons Press**
Mesa, Arizona | 2021

FIRST EDITION

Murder at the Joshua Tree
A Desert Mystery

Copyright © 2021 by Ron McCoy

Published by Many Seasons Press
(An Imprint of MultimediaPublishingProject.com)
PO Box 50553
Mesa, AZ 85208
480.939.9689 | ManySeasonsPress.com

Cover & book interior designed by Yolie Hernandez
(AZBookDesigner@icloud.com)

Front cover cabin photo by Ben Cliff (Unsplash.com)
Front and back cover photo of Joshua Trees
desert by Chelsea Bock (Unsplash.com)
Photo collage for cover created by Yolie Hernandez
(AZBookDesigner@icloud.com)

Paperback ISBN 13: 978-1-7361856-1-2
E-Book ISBN 13: 978-1-7361856-2-9

Library of Congress Control Number: 2021904073

Printed in the United States of America.

ACKNOWLEDGEMENTS

SO MANY PEOPLE HAVE PUSHED ME ALONG WITH HELP, ADVICE and encouragement. Many thanks to the *Apache Junction Writers Club*, particularly to Club President, Cathie Ringering, and fellow members John Nudge and Dick Curwin. I really appreciate Yvonne Corbett graciously lending her talent and creative input for my book. I couldn't get this into print without the expertise of Yolie Hernandez of *Many Seasons Press*. And, of course, without my wife Karen's help in writing and making resourceful changes and doing all the typing, I would be at a total loss.

TABLE OF CONTENTS

MURDER AT THE JOSHUA TREE

CHAPTER 1

IT WAS A LITTLE PAST MIDNIGHT WHEN JAKE STARTED FOR home. He was the last to leave the Show Me Later Bar and Grill. It was Saturday night and he didn't have to work the next day, Sunday, at the C-Bar Ranch. Satisfaction filled him as the bar was quiet for a Saturday night, the way he liked it. Noise made him feel claustrophobic and thinking and drinking were best done in a quiet atmosphere.

Four years ago he started working on the C-Bar Ranch in Southern Arizona. For Jake this was a positive change from working on those Colorado and Wyoming guest ranches filled with pampered women and self-centered men, neither of which could ride worth a flip and all refusing polite instructions on what they should do, even for their own safety. Results: accidents.

Winters were cold and brutal in Colorado and Wyoming where the activities changed from trail riding to snowmobiling and skiing. Jake found being a cowboy in Arizona at the C-Bar Ranch to his liking. The ranch foreman, Clem Goodman, pretty much left him alone as he did with the other two riders, Bob Bissell and Clay Robertson. They each had an area they were assigned to, where the water supply was checked along with the fences, gates, general range conditions, locating cattle and observing where they were grazing. Clem would sometimes have them work together fixing fences or moving cattle to new locations. The relentless Arizona summer heat was something to deal with, but it isn't a perfect world.

With his mind still going full speed ahead, Jake turned off the two lane blacktop. He crossed over a cattle guard and negotiated his way down a poorly graded gravel road to the ranch headquarters where no lights shown anywhere. He wound his way back to a secluded area mostly hidden by palo verde, mesquite trees and creosote bushes. There he had a twenty four foot travel trailer parked. The ranch had provided it along with air conditioning, electric and water. This was his private place. He had built a covered deck in front that provided shade along with the trees providing protection from the very occasional rains. A hammock hung under the patio roof which Jake frequently used.

He popped a can of Coors beer he'd retrieved from the refrigerator and plopping in the hammock, began drifting off to sleep, when his attention was diverted to an approaching truck moving very slowly towards his trailer. Its headlights were seeking the trailer's location. The truck stopped next to his and the driver's door opened. But the interior light didn't come on. In the darkness all he could make out was a small, slightly built figure. He called out, "Who's there?" He made sure his 9 mm was close by on the table.

"It's me, Cassie. Cassie Florence." She approached the hammock and in the moonlight Jake recognized her as the attractive girl from the Stop N Go late night service station.

"Well, this sure is a surprise," was all Jake could say as he had never seen her any place other than the Stop N Go and only talked with her then very briefly.

"Can I sit down?" she said.

"Sure, pull up that chair over there. Can I get you a drink, water or beer?"

"That would be great, but I'll get it. You look too comfortable to be disturbed. Where are the drinks?"

"They're in the refrigerator in my trailer. Excuse the mess. I don't clean anything on Saturdays and Sundays."

Cassie giggled at that and replied, "I don't either," as she returned with two beers.

Cassie appeared to be about 5'2". Petite but well proportioned. Her auburn hair was cut short, but she explained later that she grew it out longer in the winter. Her blue eyes radiated a strong will and spirit as she spoke. Jake thought that seeing her from out behind the Stop and Go counter, she was downright attractive.

"I must admit I am quite mystified by your appearance tonight." Jake said.

Cassie answered with, "You shouldn't be, Jake."

"Why is that?"

"Well, I've been flirting with you for quite a while now with no response from you whatsoever," she said. "And as you might have noticed, perhaps, the eligible men around here are very few and very far between. Unless, as a woman you like broken down cowboys with no teeth, bad breath from chewing too much tobacco with little hair on top of their head from wearing hats or caps all the time and definitely no money in their pockets. No, Jake, for some reason I see you as a different kind of person. I cornered one of your co-workers, Bob Bissell, the other day and found where you live. Sure would be nice to know you better and perhaps you might like knowing me better."

With that they talked into the night. Jake didn't elaborate or mention his past, just how he felt about things now and his past experiences with dudes and guests. Cassie expressed her disappointment in small towns with no real men or job opportunities. They ended up in the hammock together. And eventually Jake said he was done for the night and was going to call it a day and go to bed.

She responded with a shy "can I come too?"

Later that night, it had cooled off some. Jake felt her warm body next to his and pressed himself to her, appreciating the company.

Later there came a pounding on the trailer's door. "Jake, Jake!" Bob Bissell called out, "Open up, open up!"

Reluctantly Jake came to the door. "Bob, what the hell do you want?"

Bob Bissell was at least 60 and of a lean and wiry build. He was extremely bowlegged which made him look odd when he walked. He didn't shave very often, no more than once or twice a week, and seemed to always have something to talk about. He was, however, an eager and willing worker who others enjoyed working with.

"Jake, can I come in?"

"Why?"

"Oh I don't know. I just wanted to know who you had in there with you."

"What time is it, Bob?"

Bob answered with, "About 5:30 in the morning."

"So tell me why you are here before I shoot you with this gun in my hand."

"No, Jake. Clem sent me. It's the Princess. She wants to see you like right now, quick." With that Bob sprinted to his truck and left with no further explanations.

CHAPTER 2

WHILE JAKE DRESSED, CASSIE HARDLY STIRRED. HE stepped out into the still dark dawn. Lights were on at the barn and the foreman's house as he drove slowly by headed for the Princess' palatial California ocean side styled home. He had never really met Sylvia before, who was also referred to as the Princess as she was only 27 years old and lived a very private life. She had inherited the ranch from her father, Robert Simmons, some ten years ago. He had had a massive heart attack and there were no other relatives.

The C-Bar ranch had been started about 80 years before by C.J. Simmons. It is located in the southern part of Arizona and it wasn't by any stretch of the imagination the best place to build a ranch. But land was cheap, leases easily obtained and there was a lot of unclaimed land just to be used. The key was water. C.J. found five good watering holes and wells on almost 100,000 acres of land. He secured the wells and watering holes by buying the land surrounding them.

When C.J. passed away, the ranch went to his son Robert who was a skilled rancher and more importantly a sharp businessman and investor. Most of the C-Bar income came from these profitable investments in stocks and bonds of which very few people were aware.

When Robert passed away ten years before, he had already hired Carson Smith as his ranch manager. Carson, however, had almost no knowledge of the ranching business but was an outstanding numbers man. So the investments continued to flow cash. This aspect of things Jake was unaware of and really didn't care.

Sylvia seemingly had no interest in anything. She exercised in the home gym, swam in the pool and had a few friends with whom she visited in Tucson or they came to the ranch. Occasionally Sylvia took a trip to, where, nobody seemed to know or took an interest.

The house was all lit up upon his arrival. The front door was opened by Juanita, the housekeeper, before he reached it. She greeted him with a bright smile knowing exactly who he was, which surprised him as he didn't ever remember meeting her before. She ushered him into the back of the house where Sylvia was reclining on a chase lounge pool-side. She was wearing a very sheer white formfitting pair of pants and a blouse that allowed sight of everything she had on underneath or not wearing. "Jake!" she said. "I'm glad you came up so quickly on such short notice. Can we get you something to drink? Like coffee, tea or maybe something from the bar?"

Knowing his place he politely refused. At that she smiled, endeared by his modesty.

Jake at this point was completely mystified as to what was going on. He sat down in a recliner, relaxed and even closed his eyes.

Sylvia startled Jake by calling his name lifting him from his deep thoughts. "Hey, Jake! Did I wake you? You must have had a big night last night," she said with a light laugh. "We've got a serious problem. Some people are lost somewhere either on our ranch or our neighbors to the East on the Lazy 6 Ranch. I've told the Lazy 6 people we would have everyone out looking for these people this morning. You, Bob, Clay and Clem will ride in specific areas leaving as early as you can this morning."

"Jake, I want you to ride to the Joshua tree and cabin area to the far West. Look for tracks and cattle too. Once at the cabin, ride in ever widening circles looking for our lost hikers. As you know, there are so many deep arroyos a four wheel drive vehicle can't make. Going on horseback is the only way to go. It will take all day to get there, so prepare to spend the night. It's the most remote place on the ranch. Nobody goes there and no one has seen cattle there in years."

Jake interrupted. "Wait a minute. Who is missing and who would attempt a hike in the middle of summer? It's likely to be 111 or 112 degrees today."

With some hesitation Sylvia told him it was the Lazy 6 owner, Milt Powers and his wife Mildred. Then she added, "And also Carson Smith and his wife Joan."

"They went on an overnight hike?" Jake asked.

"So they say."

"Starting where?" He questioned.

"About 20 miles east of us," she said.

"On the Lazy 6?" he asked.

"Yeah, starting at their No. 1 well." she replied.

"Sylvia, none of this makes any sense, but you're the boss."

"Jake, I understand that there is a well at the Joshua tree and cabin," she replied. "So, start the aero motor windmill and, hopefully, it will pump enough water to fill the stock tank. I am told the water tastes pretty good there, too."

Jake slowly took all of this in. He was one to follow orders, but he did question her as to who was going to take care of chores tonight.

"I am," she replied. Clem will show me what to do.

Jake just looked at her and said, "Oh."

She further explained in general how to get to the Joshua tree and cabin and that Clem would explain more in detail.

He drove back to his trailer to drop his truck off at home, then he remembered Cassie and went inside to tell her what was going on.

"You're going to be gone for a couple days." She stated. "I don't have to work for a couple of days. Can I stay here? I've got nothing going on and I'm too broke to do anything."

Jake thought for a moment. He really didn't like his privacy invaded at all, but he relented. "OK, but don't mess anything up. OK? Here are a couple of 20's. Pick up a couple of steaks to grill when I get back and a big bottle of Chardonnay. You know the brand and the size, the stuff the old retired people buy."

Cassie came over to him and with tears in her eyes kissed Jake tenderly. He could only think, what's happening here?

With dawn now beginning to show early morning rays of light Jake reluctantly hurried to the barn to get his horses ready. Clem Goodman was the only person around and he had saddled Sage, a 15.1 hand steel gray gelding of some 1,100 pounds. Sage was not from Jake's regular string but that of Clem's.

"For a trip like this you'll need the best. He'll fill the bill," was Clem's only comment.

Clem was a long haired, handlebar mustachioed character. He was bowlegged and gimpy. But as foreman of the C-Bar ranch for many years he was unsurpassed. Knowing how to handle men, horses, cattle and dumb ranch managers of which Carson Smith proved to be.

When it came to improvements, Carson always found the cheapest way to do anything. The cheaper, poorly made corrals always fell apart after some usage. The smaller pens and corrals always required extra help when working cattle or horses. The old and underpowered used trucks and tractors were always breaking down. Clem managed to slip a lot of these shortcomings past him as Carson didn't come out of the office very often.

Clem said to Jake, "I've got Dewey all packed up in the corral. He'll carry anything you want and if you need to ride him, he's the best." Dewey was a 14.4 hand bay quarter horse that was also from Clem's string and Jake had ridden him a couple of times before.

Jake said to Clem, "I don't understand anything about what's going on. Why am I being sent to a far distant place I've never been to before and may likely never find on my own? How come the Princess didn't send you? You've been there before. Who's covering my area? Bob and Clay are riding theirs."

"Well, hold on," Clem said with a twinkle in his eye. "I didn't get sent frankly because I'm too old and probably in this heat would never make it, so I'm riding your area. Speaking of heat it will be 110 degrees today and it's in the middle of summer."

"Who in their right mind would go for an overnight hike?" was Jake's response."

"Well, those jaybirds don't stir about much outside and away from their air conditioning during the day. They get fooled by cool mornings and nights," was Clem's only answer.

The directions and the situation were discussed again. Clem hoped it was workable and if things got touchy, he suggested that Jake take a break and head for home, rationing the water that he carried. With that Jake swung into the saddle, grabbed Dewey's lead rope and set off with many reservations and a lot of unanswered questions.

CHAPTER 3

AS JAKE HEADED OUT, IT WAS ALREADY PRETTY HOT AND sweat began to run down his back. A GPS and compass were the only guidance items he carried. The GPS was not too helpful, not knowing the cabin's coordinates. For now hot and dry were the highlights of the day. The rains that had fallen a couple of months ago had made the now cinnamon colored bleached grass grow to new heights. The heat and sun dried the blades so badly, that as the horse's hooves struck the grass the blades shattered and fell to the desert floor. The very occasional ironwood and palo verde trees were stunted from heat and lack of water, thereby offering little shade. The even now normally healthy cacti appeared to be more scattered and less dense.

The sky was a very pale white blue and the sun beat down relentlessly. Finding many low hills, a great number of large rocks and deep arroyos that were abundant made it easy for Jake to see why vehicles couldn't cross this land. Time after time he had to work for alternate routes to find his way. Dust clung to the sweat that covered both horses and rider giving them a ghostly look from the past. They stopped in the early afternoon. However, nowhere was there any shade. They drank their allotted share of water. Jake could only hope for water at their destination, but began to sincerely doubt that there would be any place as remote as this area. It was barren, inhospitable and likely nobody had been here in years.

At this point he seriously considered turning around, however, without changing his plans, he rode a little further to see if he could find the cabin. If he did find it, he'd turn around and come straight back the next day. Other than that, if he didn't find the cabin today he would stop at dusk and turn around and head back.

Jake felt that he was wrapped in some kind of highly heated substance. The air was so thick and hot it was hardly breathable. He felt that he had to push his way through the air, however, he and his two horses continued to move forward. They knew they had a duty and a job to do, but in this heat they were clearly risking their own lives. The desert before him was bleached to a somber almost colorless hue.

Jake was his own man and very quiet. He didn't speak badly about anybody or anything on the few occasions when he did talk. He knew that wasn't the way he had always been. Well-built for his 5' 8" stature and with a hint of gray beginning to show in his dark brown hair, at 34 girls still seemed to find him attractive in a youthful way. Nonetheless, as he thought about it, he was surprised he and Cassie talked as much as they did last night. He knew how reserved he was. Having things quiet around him gave him time to think and sort things out. He liked being alone.

Jake didn't feel like killing himself on a wild goose chase. And certainly had a lot of cause to wonder about some of the things that were happening. Why had Sylvia specifically told him where to search? Had she talked to Clay or Bob? How was it that she seemed to know exactly the location of the cabin? He thought her last statement to him was rather strange. 'Look all around you real good and see if anything looks out of place'.

Their pace had slowed with the intense heat. He frequently had to change directions as a result of deep arroyos, rocky hillsides and in some places dense cactus and vegetation. He stopped again to water the horses and get a drink for himself. There was no shade to be found anywhere. The horses' sweat created a glossy sheen and in some places began to dry on their coats. His shirt was soaked through and even after getting a good drink, felt a little light headed and certainly dehydrated. Again he was thinking of just quitting and turning around and heading back. He really didn't understand any of this but he always followed orders and continued on his way.

Clem had told him he would eventually come to a dried river bed on which the opposite side was a thirty to forty foot dirt wall, turn left and then ride in the riverbed, after a mile or so you will come to a gap. Ride through that and you'll see the cabin in the distance.

By late afternoon they were really feeling stressed out and finally came to a dry river bed and the dirt wall he figured Clem was talking about. Turning left, he rode a short ways and came to the gap. They crested the gap and the Joshua tree and the cabin came into view. With great relief he rode to the cabin.

CHAPTER 4

NOT MUCH WAS IN THE CABIN. IT WAS JUST A ONE ROOM frame building. No door, no glass in the windows, an old steel bed and was completely empty otherwise with a dirt floor. No corrals, pens or fence that left anything to tie a horse to except an old tired and worn windmill. The windmill basin was about half full with fairly clear water and only a small amount of algae floated on the surface. They all tanked up on the water. Jake released the brake on the windmill and a light wind pushed and cajoled the sails to move and slowly turn. The sucker rod began to dip down, cranking and creaking but finally began to bring up water. Jake filled the twelve foot wide cement tank to overflowing and now had plenty of water for his outfit for several days. He unsaddled the horses, fed pellets and grain, and tied them by their halters to the support rails of the windmill.

During his ride to the cabin, he saw no tracks of any kind and nothing seemed out of place. The barren desert was devoid of any wildlife or stock of any kind. Only wildlife seemingly came to the water tank. But who had turned on the windmill so that the tank was actually about half full at this time? Somebody had been here before him recently. And why did Sylvia give him instructions and to him only rather than to Clem the foreman? He now knew things weren't right at all.

He opened a can of pears for himself along with a can of Vienna Sausages. Sometime was spent looking for a place to spread his bedroll, however, the bed in the cabin seemed to be the best option. Snakes, spiders and scorpions were to be avoided as bedfellows at all cost.

Morning came after an uneventful night. A can of spam was opened for breakfast. More pellets and grain rationed for his two horses. He didn't get into too much of a hurry knowing already that this would be an uneventful day. But he would follow his instructions, riding in ever widening circles looking for tracks, signs of cattle and anything unusual. Once mounted, Jake set off. The sun was already bearing down from a cloudless sky. Shade wasn't there for a rider on a horse and the sparse vegetation didn't offer much in the way of feed for any livestock or wildlife for that matter.

Sweat rolled off his forehead and covered his back. He was riding Dewey now and had made three very large circles before lunch and headed back to the famous Joshua tree and cabin as he thought of it now. Resting for a couple of hours and cooling off in the stock tank, Jake saddled up Sage taking even more water with him and a collapsible pail for Sage to drink from when he stopped. He never saw anything during the afternoon and had made two full circles and was about ten miles from the tree and camp.

As the afternoon began to come to a close, it was then that he saw in the distance ten to twelve turkey vultures circling in the sky. Too many for just a rabbit he thought and he headed in that direction to check it out. After 45 minutes of riding he came upon what the turkey vultures were after. In a wash there lay the bodies of two men. They had been shot and he recognized them both; Carson Smith and Milt Powers. Jake knew he couldn't do much of anything other than to try to cover them with some of the packed canvas they had used to travel with. This was clearly just a temporary fix as there were likely to be too many predators. He covered them the best he could, gathering some rocks to hold the tarps down. This was his only choice. There was no way that he could pack the bodies back.

He took out the GPS and recorded the coordinates of the location. From there he rode back to the cabin and fed the horses. He poured water over the horses to try to get rid of as much of the dried sweat from their bodies as he could and brushed them down thoroughly. Then he stripped off his clothes, jumped into the stock tank pulling his clothes after him, swished them around to rinse them off and then hung them on the side of the stock tank to dry. He relaxed in the water for a while feeling extremely refreshed from his ordeal of two days of riding in the heat. A trip to the Show Me Later Bar and Grill in town was in order. He had some serious drinking to do.

Night closed in on him and the moon lit his way about the camp. The evening air closed in on him and he felt refreshed, but he was extremely tired and couldn't rationalize what was going on. He stretched out on the bed expecting to fall asleep quickly, but his mind was so filled with questions of which any answers weren't going to happen any time soon. Why were Carson and Milt separated from their wives? Jake knew that even though both ranches consisted of large acreages, neither man spent much time outside their offices. They were apparently very lost and travelling in a very remote area with miles of nothing ahead of them. Probably miles from their drop-off point. Unfortunately for them, they did not know they were going in the totally wrong direction.

Someone had been coming here off and on as the windmill did work and someone had kept most of the algae in the tank cleaned up. He had been told getting here by horseback was the only way and after yesterday's ride he felt the same way. So how did the well get drilled and how did the cement for the stock tank get here? What about the building materials for the cabin? Many pieces were too big to be packed in. The biggest mystery to Jake was why the cabin was built here in the first place.

He now knew there must be a way to get a truck back here. With this all turning about in his mind, sleep finally overtook him.

CHAPTER 5

J AKE DIDN'T GET THE PREDAWN START HE WANTED, BUT TOOK very little time packing up the two horses, taking everything back with him. He figured his return trip should go faster as he could follow his tracks and had the GPS to keep him on course. He swung into the saddle now riding Dewey as he seemed fresher and more rested. He was very anxious to report his findings to Sheriff Wayne Rogers.

Another heat infused day was in the making. As the day progressed heat waves shimmered ahead of him, tempting any water starved man or beast that there was water ahead. Prickly pear, cholla and saguaro cactus lined the way with a sprinkling of palo verde, ironwood and mesquite. Concentrating on his route he felt he was making good progress. Striking off in a general direction can be somewhat chancy. However, he stuck to his route and felt that this was the best way to get back to the ranch. Then in the distance he saw something reflecting sunlight, not too far ahead of him.

Soon he saw the gold reflection before him on the desert floor looking like a brilliant candy wrapper. Sylvia's instruction crossed his mind, 'Look for things that seem out of place'. Certainly this candy wrapper was out of place as nobody had been across this stretch of desert in a very long time. He would have been less amazed if it had been an old Colt 45. Then Jake's eye caught three sets of footprints going away from civilization and headed to nowhere. He then turned and followed them taking him away from his desired destination and route.

The footprints were hard to follow. Wind had erased some stretches. In other places the footprints disappeared when crossing solid rock. But by midmorning he came upon the three women he was tracking. They were in life threatened condition. He barely recognized Mildred Powers and Joan Smith with their swollen, sun burnt and blistered faces and arms. Mildred was on the verge of total collapse. The third, a woman who looked to be in her late 20's and was totally unknown to him. The only comfort he had was water, of which they had none. The fact that someone, anyone, had come along revitalized them considerably. When he told them they were headed straight into nowhere, they didn't believe him. "No, no! The C-Bar ranch could only be one or two miles in the direction that we are heading." The three of them said in unison.

Jake's reply was unconvincing. "The C-Bar ranch head-quarters is still a very long way off. I know. I work there and am heading back there. I also know exactly where I am," which wasn't totally true. "Mildred, I'll put you on my horse. Joan, you get on the pack horse. I will take off all the gear, except the water. I'll mark the location on my GPS. Your friend and I will walk."

That was a great idea but the fact that Mildred was somewhat overweight, diabetic and very opinionated made getting her on a horse was a challenge. But with Lois' help and a horse willing to stand still through all this nonsense, they got her on. Jake realized Mildred seemed to be fading fast and was close to unconsciousness.

Jake knew that it would likely be nightfall before they would reach the C-Bar ranch. Things went well for a while, but Mildred was totally out of it. Before long, he had to walk beside the horse just to keep her on. The third woman in the group said her name was Lois and she was a photographer. She had been invited by Mildred, whom she said she had been acquainted with for some time. However, she had lost her photo equipment along the way. She was younger than the others including Jake and seemingly very fit, but even she was now beginning to falter.

Jake called for a short break in a shade free area. The water was pretty warm, but reviving, as all of them were in dire need of hydration. Joan had gotten off Dewey and collapsed on the ground. Mildred toppled off Sage unconscious with Lois barely able to cushion her fall. Jake knew he'd never get her back on Sage and decided he'd have to ride for help. He tried his cell phone at this point but still no signal.

They were now located in a four wheel drive accessible area. Finally getting a GPS location, he unloaded everything he had leaving all of it with the women. Mildred was still unconscious. Joan raved that they were going in the wrong direction. Lois was the only rational one. Jake made her promise to stay where they were and to keep the other two women near her. He told Lois that it would likely take him two hours to get to the ranch, but driving back would be pretty fast. He set off riding Sage and ponying Dewey. Both horses were pretty well spent.

Two hours later he arrived at the ranch to find Sylvia doing evening chores. "Get the Sheriff out here quick! I found Milt and Carson and they've been shot fatally. Here's the GPS location. I need the jeep to go back and get the three women. Better have an ambulance here as Mildred is unconscious."

Sylvia was on the phone with the Sheriff's office as Jake drove off in a cloud of dust. Shortly he was at the scene where he had left the three women and was relieved to find them still there. As they loaded up, Lois said that Joan kept wandering off babbling to herself 'Chee nu'. Mildred now appeared to have passed away while he was gone. Her overweight and lifeless body was a challenge for Jake and Lois to load into the jeep. Returning back to the C-Bar ranch in an air conditioned vehicle was a relief for everyone. Joan even stopped babbling for a while.

The EMT's loaded the occasionally babbling Joan and lifeless Mildred into the ambulance, stabilizing Joan somewhat, but they could not revive Mildred. They left with lights blazing in a clearly visible hurry.

Sheriff Rogers hadn't arrived yet, but darkness had fallen on the C-Bar ranch. There probably wasn't much anyone could do until daylight. Lois now refreshed with more water was considerably revived.

"Jake," she said. "I'd like to go over to the Lazy 6 and get my jeep. It's got most of my stuff in it. I left my camera back on the trail when Mildred started needing more help, and I'd like to find it before the sun cooks it another day."

Jake passed her over to Clem who then asked his hand, Bob, to take her over to the Lazy 6. In the morning Bob could help her find her camera equipment.

Jake's mind really began wandering now. He needed a shower, a change of clothes and a trip to the Show Me Later Bar and Grill, thinking and drinking. At his trailer from the outside he noted Cassie's barely running Datsun pickup truck parked in front. The trailer lights were on. Inside it was unusually neat and clean. Cassie was in his recliner reading a Tony Hillerman mystery book that she had found in his bookshelf. He questioned Cassie. "Did you ever go home?" with a happy glint in his eye.

"No, Jake." Setting the book aside her answer continued. "I didn't feel like going to my very boring apartment. Hope you don't mind, but if you are done with me that's Okay. I know I've intruded in your space."

"That you have," was his reply, "but I'm not looking for any kind of explanation now, how about a trip to the bar?"

She smiled at that. "But what about those steaks you asked me to get?"

He replied, "We'll do them tomorrow night as I feel we'll be spending a lot of time with the sheriff's department tomorrow."

At the Show Me Later Cassie pointed out that Manuel apparently had been doing well. The bar had been completely upgraded and the solid four inch oak bar top was impressive in this out-of-the way place. It now seated some 25 people more than the former ten or so at one time. The early evening crowd was surprisingly light, but it wasn't the snowbird season yet. The somewhat smaller dining room seating some thirty customers had also been upgraded. Murals on the wall highlighted by colorful Mexican tiles were inlaid into the wall and also into the archways. Manuel had always been blessed with the same kitchen help and seemingly was never understaffed. The patio that could seat some fifty or more people was a perfect place for a delightful Mexican dinner.

The patio was surrounded with a seven foot adobe wall with tile and river rock artistically inlaid. The patio side next to the main restaurant was raised several feet allowing the patrons a scenic view of purple colored mountains rising some thirty miles away. Pristine natural desert stretched to the mountains unimpeded. Only mesquite and palo verde trees created a dimension to the scene with the seemingly ever present saguaro cactus. The smooth cement floor was painted a polished mahogany. The avocado colored walls were trimmed with turquoise created highlights. Murals decorated the walls, along with ornate framed mirrors.

One of the things Jake liked about this place was the various choices of seating. He usually sat at the bar enjoying the companionship of other serious drinkers. The dining room was quieter, the TV less loud, and also a better place than the patio when weather was an issue. Now, the patio dimly lit was perfect for a romantic interlude.

This is where Jake steered Cassie. He was glad he'd had a chance to clean up and felt refreshed and ready for a good meal. They casually ordered drinks and dinner. He surprised Cassie by ordering a bottle of Pinot Noir wine. She had always thought he was just a beer drinking cowboy. One more new thing she was finding out about him.

She also now realized that there was something a whole lot more to this man than she ever thought or realized. After some small talk, Cassie really relaxed, even though Jake was obviously filled with thought.

"These last few days," he stated, "Why did these two couples decide to go camping in the middle of summer? Why not at the ranches up in Colorado, where it is cooler? And from what I understand they had done that before."

Cassie having not been filled in on any of this looked at him perplexed as he went on saying, "Who the hell is this Lois, the photographer? Where did she come from? The sheriff needs to catch up with her and ask where she fits into this whole scenario. Why did Sylvia call me to her house to give me instructions? Clem knows the area better than me and likely better than her, so why didn't he tell me how to find this place in the beginning of all of this?"

"Well, Jake, it's not your problem. You did what the bosses told you to do. So let the proper authorities figure it out. You've done everything right, so let it go."

"I guess you're right," replied Jake. "So, tell me Cassie have you gone back to work yet?"

Cassie hesitated and had trouble finding her voice. "Jake, I have a problem there. The owner of the Stop and Go decided that the third shift was not profitable. The guy on that shift had been with them for a long time, so they laid me off and put him to running my shift."

Surprised, Jake just looked at her and asked, "When did that happen?"

"Well," she said, "A week or so ago."

"So, what are you going to do now?"

She said, "That's a problem. I didn't have enough money to pay the rent on my apartment, so I gave it up and moved out. I spent a few days in my truck and I guess I then barged into your life. I'm sorry that I didn't tell you what was really going on."

"Well," he said, "I know that jobs are few and far between and with this murder scenario we are going to be tied up for a while. We'll worry about your future after Sheriff Wayne Rogers gets everything all cleared up. So, just stay in the trailer with me for now."

CHAPTER 6

CASSIE MADE HAM, POTATOES AND EGGS FOR THEM THE NEXT morning. Jake assumed things, though problematic at this time, a normalcy would return to his life and he could be a cowboy again. So today, Tuesday, he reported to work. Clem was confused or just not sure of what to do when he showed up. He started with telling Jake, Bob and Clay to do a few chores around the barn just for today as the Sheriff would be around wanting to ask a lot of questions.

"One of you needs to reshoe Gray Spot and Silver. Then there are two bridles that need to be overhauled. You know, the ones we set aside a couple of months ago. And some of those older used saddles could use some cleaning up. We will see how things develop today."

"Jake, if that gal you are seeing needs something to do, send her up. My wife could use some help with Joan and keeping track of everybody coming and going. Joan is still babbling 'chee nu'.

Midday, Clem confided with the crew that Sheriff Wayne had flown out to the murder site in a department helicopter. The medical examiner had found nothing new or significant, nor did the crime scene investigator. The bodies of Carson Smith and Milt Powers had been recovered. Clem added that Mildred Powers had been pronounced dead upon arrival at the hospital. The cause of death was unknown pending the coroner's autopsy. The Sheriff was at a loss as to how all of this happened in such a remote area, but he was really upset that the photographer Lois had apparently vanished as she was nowhere to be found. He had an all-points bulletin out for her arrest, but he only had a limited description of her vehicle.

Sylvia caught up with Clem just outside of his house in one of her rare appearances outside of her compound. "Clem, I've looked at our finances and can't make heads or tails out of it. I can't even find what the ranch checking account has in it or my own checking account, for that matter. Milt was in charge of all of our finances for us for so many years. Even when dad was still with us, he always did such a wonderful job of taking care of everything. I need help and don't know where to find it. I don't want any of those local number dummies to know anything about our finances."

Clem thought for a moment. "You know you've got a guy right here that could help you."

"He's right here on the ranch, but is about a private a man as I know. When I hired him and asked him what he had done in the past, he told me he had graduated from The University of Illinois with a degree in accounting and financial investments."

"That could only be Jake, right?"

"Yeah."

"If you would, Clem, have him come to my house as soon as possible."

"He's riding the South range today, but I expect him in around two o'clock when it's definitely too hot to be out there."

Jake got in by early afternoon and was in the shade of the barn, brushing down his mount Lucky, when Clem approached him. "Jake," he said. "Sylvia wants to see you right away."

"What's all that about?" he asked.

"Ask her," was Clem's reply.

Juanita smiled as she opened the door for Jake and ushered him to Sylvia's main office in the Big House. After a little small talk Sylvia said, "I am mystified by all of these events, Jake. Obviously, nothing makes any sense at all. So I want to see where you found Milt and Carson. Then I want to see where you found the three women. I also want to find where they camped and maybe find Lois's camera equipment. So, how about leaving at four in the morning tomorrow and going straight to the Joshua tree and the cabin? I know a route that may be a little shorter. Maybe there is something we have missed in all of this."

Jake then spent the afternoon packing for an overnight trip thinking now that she knows a short cut, the ride out and back should be a lot faster. He would also then know the way on the return trip if anything out of the ordinary should happen. He took care to pack his Smith & Wesson .38 caliber revolver in a very accessible place.

That night with Cassie Jake grilled T-bone steaks and baked Patsy potatoes. Rolls and coleslaw were added to the menu. A bottle of chilled Pinot Noir wine appeared from nowhere. Jake had told Cassie about the upcoming trip tomorrow.

Upon learning this, Cassie was frustrated, but kept it to herself. Was Jake her man or was he Sylvia's? She had only been with Jake for four days. She realized that Sylvia was probably unknowingly challenging her for his attention. Cassie was thinking that maybe she just wouldn't be there when they came back, feeling it was time for him to make a move. The steak dinner was done with flair and eagerness and was totally mesmerizing. Was he playing her or was this the man he really was? Again, she realized Jake had a lot of mystery behind him.

CHAPTER 7

I T WAS FOUR AM THE NEXT MORNING WHEN SYLVIA JOINED HIM at the barn to pack up the horses. Dewey, his preferred pack horse, was destined to be the carrier of the goods they were taking. Sylvia watched Jake for a few moments as he with his pannier scale weighed each pack item and divided them into two packs.

"Jake, you are a trip and a half. I didn't even know you could pack a horse at all."

"Comes with time," was his reply.

He thought to himself, well, you just do what the boss wants you to do. After all, she is paying the bills. He expertly threw a diamond hitch over the now balanced load that was within a half a pound of being equal. Since this was for one night only and plenty of water was available at the cabin, the pack load for Dewey was relatively light.

Sylvia expertly saddled her horse, a seven year old chestnut Arab and Jake again took Sage for his mount. They got off in good time with Sylvia leading the way. Even in the predawn darkness, she knew where she was going. Dawn soon came and the day became warm and then hot. They traveled well in the early morning, but by noon time the temperature was at least 110 degrees. The horses slowed some under the heat. Jake sweated through his shirt and the dust stirred up from the horse hooves settled on the two riders and three horses.

By midafternoon they had arrived at the Joshua tree and cabin. The stock tank was still relatively full and the horses and riders drank their fill. Jake with Sylvia unsaddled the horses and set up camp. Sylvia then stood on the side of the cement tank, stripped off all of her clothes and jumped in the stock tank. Oh well, Jake thought, I'm hot, sweaty and dusty and followed suit. They swished their clothes around in the water and then hung them on the windmill tower to dry.

He asked Sylvia "You've been here a lot before, haven't you?"

She smiled, "How could you guess."

"There is another way to get here."

"Why do you say that?"

"Well, for starters the cement for this stock tank couldn't be hauled in with horses, nor could the lumber for the cabin or the windows. A truck brought all this stuff in and you know where the trail is, right?"

"Right." was Sylvia's only response.

They talked into the night about her life and his life cowboying. When they turned in for the night, she said, "I know all about that girl in your trailer, but this is tonight."

They shared the old fashioned iron and steel spring bed. Both of them were keenly aware of visiting rattle snakes and numerous scorpions. Therefore, sleeping on the cabin floor or on the ground outside had little appeal

Jake, drawing from his experience taking people out on pack trips, had easily prepared a stew last night and this morning whipped up omelets and coffee on a small one burner camp stove. She saddled up the horses while he cleaned up from breakfast.

They set off in good time leading Dewey as they didn't want to leave him at the cabin. He'd likely wear himself out pacing back and forth, looking for the other horses. In just over an hour and a half they arrived at the crime scene. There was no sign whatsoever of what had happened there. The ever present light wind had erased every sign of tracks or presence of anyone being there earlier, including the Sheriff, his crew and the county helicopter.

Sylvia walked around thoughtfully taking it all in. "I guess I just wanted to see where they came to an end. I just can't believe it. I can't even imagine how or why. I'm going to climb up on that high ridge over there on the edge of this arroyo and say good-bye to them and this area. Don't plan on ever coming back again, including to that damn Joshua tree and cabin. I'll return shortly Jake. Please just wait here."

He saw her sitting on the ridge, still. Not moving. After almost two hours she returned. She'd been crying, he noticed, but said nothing. Checking the cinches they mounted up and rode back to the Joshua tree and the cabin. There they packed up everything they had brought with them and headed back to the C-Bar Ranch.

The sun was out in full force now, virtually baking them. It sweat soaked their clothes and the dust kicked up by the horses settled on them. The terrain was rocky, broken by many arroyos and small ridges which made for many uphill and downhill climbs. Cactus, brittle bush, mesquite, ironwood and palo verde created an obstacle course for them to wind their way through. On a cool day this whole experience might have been pleasant; however, they rode silently for the most part with Sylvia leading the way. After a couple of hours, they stopped for a moment giving the horses a short drink from the water they carried. They made good time getting back to the C-Bar Ranch where Jake unpacked Dewey and sorted all of their gear into canvas packed covers.

Bob had come out of the bunkhouse and unsaddled Sage for him. He proceeded to hose Sage off at the wash rack.

Sylvia and her chestnut gelding, Coco, were at the wash rack by that time. She and Bob talked amicably. Jake, surprised at their familiarity, wondered if Bob had ever met Sylvia.

When she left after turning her horse out, Jake asked Bob if he knew her from before. Bob replied, "Nope. First time I ever saw her. And, wow! Good looking, ain't she?"

For all that sunburned skin and dust covered sweaty clothes Jake thought that was quite a compliment toward Sylvia. He and Bob put the horses up and put their gear back into the tack room.

Back at his trailer he found Cassie. He showered and shaved and put on clean clothes that somehow had gotten ironed. "Let's go the Show Me Later. I need to do some thinking and drinking. We'll have some food, too."

"Sounds good to me," she said. "And I've got something to talk to you about."

Manuel was busy as usual although his place was not. They were welcomed with a smile by the one and only waitress. They seated themselves on the patio raised deck to watch the evening sunset over the purple colored mountains. Pinot Noir wine was served to him and a Corona Light for her. She ordered a burrito with rice and beans. He settled for a stuffed enchilada. He told her most of what happened at the Joshua tree and the cabin.

She said, "I've been helping Clem's wife take care of things, particularly with Joan. She was still out of her mind babbling 'Chee nu'. I finally sat with her and asked her who is Chee nu? She looked at me and said, 'No, no not a person. Mildred knew that someone was trying to kill her'. I asked her, "Who?" She either didn't know or didn't want to tell me. Then she seemed relieved and didn't babble anymore. Do you think we should call the Sheriff?"

"You bet," Jake responded. He then dialed the Sheriff's office. The Sheriff was out, but Jake talked to the chief deputy, who was intensely interested in this development. He said they would be out early tomorrow morning to talk to Joan. He specifically asked for Cassie to be there also, hoping she'd lend a calming effect with Joan.

Cassie made breakfast for them; pancakes and sausage. Jake noted someone must have gone to the grocery store, so he asked, "Are you planning on moving in here?"

Cassie replied, "All you have to do is give me the word. But I won't play second fiddle to that bitch. I know she's the boss and you're just one of the ranch hands. Why, with all her money and high society friends, she'd easily find somebody in the glitz and glamour circles. From what I see in you, Jake, the glitz and high society is not your forte, right? Ha! Really, we've only known each other for just a week. Just seeing you and observing you before that night I came here, well, that doesn't count?"

He responded, "Cassie, you're special. Easily a person I want to know better and be with. This week with you has been very special to me. Sadly with three murders in all of this, I have not given you any of the respect and attention you deserve. So, move in here with me in this luxurious twenty four foot travel trailer. Maybe Clem will give you some kind of a job here on the ranch. Let's find out who we are in the hammock, tonight, with some Pinot Noir and we'll discover each other."

The next day, Jake said to Cassie, "Lots of happening here today with the Sheriff coming out and I'm supposed to meet with Bitch sometime today."

They went to Carson and Joan's house. Clem's wife had been looking after Joan since her ordeal and was extremely relieved having Cassie's help. They sat and visited with coffee until the arrival of Sheriff Wayne Rogers and his crew.

Sheriff Wayne Rogers was a very experienced and resourceful law man. He had been sheriff for a good number of years and appeared to be in his late 40's. He was always dressed very well, in great physical shape and was easily 6 feet tall. He had a relaxed air about him and was quick to smile. He was seldom challenged by anyone including some pretty tough offenders of the law. He easily recognized that this interview would require much patience and time with the overall objective of collecting information. Jake did ask what the autopsy and Coroner's report stated.

"Can't comment on very much of this subject, but it appears that the insulin in her system was significantly insufficient, so that with dehydration and exhaustion, coupled with the heat which caused her system to cease functioning."

"What happened to her proper dosage of any medicines?" Jake then asked if any of the doctor prescribed medication had been looked at.

"We are looking at that as we speak."

"Have all of her bottles of medications been checked for usage and quality?"

"Another reason we are here," said the Sheriff. "Certainly with what apparently Mildred told Joan, someone was trying to kill her. We need to collect all of these items and question everybody thoroughly, so we'll be interviewing everybody here whether they knew Mildred or not. So we'll be starting with you two, Jake and Cassie."

Cassie didn't have much to offer as she had only been coming to the ranch for about a week. She did, however, get Joan to explain her 'Chee nu' babbling.

Jake went over all of what happened to him which was extensive and he voiced his concerns. Why did Sylvia give him instructions to go out to the cabin rather than Clem? He was told that the route to the cabin was only by horseback. Later to discover that there was a motorized route. Apparently, that had been used a long time ago, likely many years ago. Why did Sylvia want to go on an overnight trip to the murder scene? She had admitted to Jake that she had been there before and seemed to have an emotional investment in being there. No tracks or signs were found at the site. Why? It was anybody's guess.

When Sheriff Rogers finished talking with Jake, Jake left and went to the main house to talk to Sylvia. She was dressed differently than he had seen before; tight jeans, crisp pressed western blouse. They sat down with coffee. "Jake, you sure are different from anyone I've met before. You know what you like and what you don't. Why being a cowboy on the C-Bar Ranch fills you with satisfaction, well, I don't understand that."

After some more small talk about what all was going on with Sheriff Rogers, Sylvia stated, "Jake, before we rode to the cabin, I talked to Clem about you. He revealed to me that you have not been a cowboy all of your life. And, in fact, you had graduated from the University of Illinois with a degree in accounting. This only substantiated the fact that I have always felt that you have a past that we have not heard anything about, so I googled you on my computer. I didn't expect to find much as you're not the rich and famous. Oh! Here's a graduation picture from college. You sure looked a lot younger then. That was, what, eleven years ago? I guess the years are not good for our looks. It says here you joined your father's firm in Chicago."

She suddenly looked at Jake and exclaimed, "Oh my God! You are *that* Jake French, eligible bachelor, playboy who disappeared some seven years ago. The magazines and scandal sheets have played up that disappearance for years. Is it true you graduated from the University of Illinois with a Master's Degree in Accounting and you had then joined, apparently, your father's accounting and investment firm in Chicago?"

"Jake, do you care to enlighten me about this? It's very important to me."

With that Jake became very reflective and quiet, got up, walked around the room some and said finally, "OK. I'll talk about it. But this is between just us."

"Well, I know I can drive a new pickup truck, three quarter ton, four wheel drive and all that, but my 12 year old Chevy runs just fine and keeps me in the reality of life. So, as I tell you all of this I can only reflect on how much better life is for me now than the way it all started."

Jake continued, "Yeah, I know having a good bit of money on the side certainly provides comfort. I do still play the investment game for that matter just for the challenge of it. Not being on a time schedule to clients and plenty of time to think things out, I have been very successful for what little time and effort I put into it."

"My father is an accountant, stock broker and investor. He created a large firm on Michigan Avenue in downtown Chicago. He, of course, expected me to follow in his footsteps. And gave me any and everything I ever wanted but in reality it was not too much. I did very well academically and also in sports while in high school. I never had my own car but had several to choose from in Dad's garage. I never thought too much about the future as I was having too much fun."

"I started at the University of Illinois Champaign Urbana College which is located in the central Illinois farming area and for me the aura of big city life began to disappear. That of rural life brought a new stimulation of thoughts and visions to me. I started dating in my freshman year of college a girl who lived on a farm in Iowa. She had a car, I did not. I don't know why but my bicycle seemed to be enough. This girl invited me to come with her every time she went home. I was enthralled with operating big equipment, picking corn and beans, and cutting, raking and baling hay. I felt renewed. My parents didn't see or comprehend what was happening to their son. They just chalked it up to *girlitis*."

"Graduating with an honors degree in Business and Accounting, I submitted to my parents' desire to join Dad's accounting firm. It wasn't too bad in the beginning. Eventually though, exacting numbers on lesser accounts while wearing expensive suits and ties seemed to drain my energy, while visits to my U of I girlfriend revitalized it. However, her occasional visits to my Chicago home left her uninspired and unmotivated and she slowly slipped away."

"I made up my mind I'd give this experience of crunching numbers five years. My parents in the meantime pushed me to date more socially prominent girls. Unfortunately, all of this pomp and circumstance left me cold for some reason. A lot of it was because these girls were so stuck on themselves and I found them to be boring. At this time, however, I guess I was considered to be a highly eligible bachelor. Those glamour magazines began to follow me and whatever date I was escorting. The final touch came when a well-known actress in California actually paid me money to accompany her to some big glitzy awards thing. This happened several more times over a year or so. Now I was some kind of playboy and Dad's investment company flourished. All I got out of it was feeling like I was a damn gigolo."

Sylvia said, "It says here you are worth $2.5 million. You must have got something out of it all."

He continued, "Four years had gone by and my mother passed away that winter. That left me with a severely grieving father to deal with. I had always lived at home, used my father's endless supply of money, cars, etc. I had a large bank account and I knew I was spoiled. It was time to move on. So I told my father in April that I wanted and needed the summer off. My father really didn't comprehend what this was all about.

"He knew and I knew that I had my nose to the proverbial grindstone and needed a break. So, with some misgiving, Dad relented saying, 'Be back by mid-September. We need you and I need you at the firm'. So, I, with a gladdened heart made plans.

46

"The internet provided me with access to buying a used pickup truck. The elderly man in a nearby town who owned it rarely drove it. His daughter kept a tight rein on her father's driving. It was a low mileage, half ton V8 extended cab with four wheel drive. I didn't see any dents or rust and it was only five years old. So I asked them if they minded if I took it to my mechanic to check it out. The daughter agreed but wanted either one of them to go with me.

"'Fine by me,' I told them.

"'Get in, Dad,' the daughter had said."

So we set off to the mechanics place. I asked the dad, "How do you feel about this and what should I call you?"

He said, "Mark, and I don't like any of this worth a crap. Sir, Sally worries about everything I do. She treats me like a seven year old."

So I asked him, "How about we drop the truck off at the mechanic and go next door to Turners Bar for a couple of beers?"

Mark told me that that was the best idea he'd heard all month. After a couple of hours, we became the best of friends. I bought a few more beers as we talked. After that I told Mark it was time to see the mechanic.

Mark was ready. "Let's go," he told me.

We found the mechanic finishing up and wiping his hands on a shop towel. He told me, "It's a steal at any price; low mileage, hardly ever out of the garage."

I wanted to verify with Mark the asking price which he restated to me.

I told Mark that it was a done deal and reached in for my wallet paying Mark in cash. Mark was astonished.

I asked him, "How will your daughter, Sally, deal with this?"

"Ha, ha!" was his answer. Saying it was her idea, not his.

Jake became somewhat reflective at this time and told Sylvia, "And you know what? Every time I go back to Chicago I always spend one afternoon with Mark at Turners Bar. He loves it."

"So with that I loaded up my truck and set off for Colorado. I didn't really say good bye at the office or say that much to my father either, but I sure felt free. On the drive I took in the spaces all around me. I thought about and wondered about the people who seemingly lived miles from anywhere as I tooled down the highway, viewing occasional houses decorated by old cars, trucks and falling down fences. Yes, there were people, but who they were and why they were there, I don't know. It wasn't for me to study about it at that time. I just rolled on by."

"The changes in the environment and scenery were something to wonder about. Across Illinois the rich farmland offered endless miles of corn, soybeans and cattle. Many of the homes were new and the older framed houses were whitewashed that apparently were owned by the same family for years."

"The changes that I saw in places like Iowa and Northern Missouri didn't change too much from what I saw in Illinois. However, Kansas is flat, windblown with crystal blue skies. The summers there are hot and my truck's AC was put to work. Lunch and supper stops were genuine treats; the small towns, Mom and Pop outfits scattered along my route. They were all inviting, but I couldn't stop at them all. The rest you pretty much know about already."

"Not all of it, Jake. How did you get a job wrangling dudes on horses with no experience?"

"I did have some experience. I rode at several stables while in Chicago as a boy and I even helped out with doing chores some. That Iowa girl had horses and we did ride together a lot."

"That's quite a story, Jake, if I say so myself. You've been here for over four years and I'd never guess that your past was so unusual to put it mildly, but then I never knew you or I might have been showing up at that hidden trailer like that bimbo who is there now. Oops! Sorry about that."

"That's OK, Sylvia, you should hear what she calls you."

"Does she know anything about your past and that bank account?"

"No, and nobody else does either and it will stay that way. I've got no ties here and can just saddle up and ride out of here on a moment's notice anytime I like."

"Just interested in cows, fences and watering holes, right?"

"Jake, I've looked at the books and the accounts and I can't make any sense out of them. Seems like a lot of money is floating around and I can't seem to make any sense of any of it. I don't trust anyone about this mess."

"Well, down to business; I need a skilled numbers dummy, bad. You fill the bill. I need someone who understands the economics of ranching and some basic management. I want to hire you to fill Carson Smith's position. I'll also retain you as a working cowboy under Clem Goodman's instructions at your current salary. I'll even pay minimum wage for that girl you have down there to take care of Joan. Here's also a new twist to the whole thing; Milt Powers' two sons are coming here on Friday to take care of their parents' remains and to decide what to do about the ranch. So, we'll need to come up with what it's really worth and how much money I do have potentially to buy it. We'll also need to make a trip to the bank to get some of those accounts in your name, so you can pay bills and wages. I need you to go over all of these accounts and financial statements. I can get them to you later today. That's what I propose. What do you think?"

Jake said, "Well, going over all of your accounts and records shouldn't take too long. I will then consider your very generous offer at that time."

"What do you think our net worth is?" Sylvia asked. "Just make a rough estimate."

"I couldn't even take a wild guess," Jake said. Then he said, "I really appreciate your offer and your confidence in me."

They then went to Carson's office and started to work on the books just after noon time. Carson's office, however, was cluttered. The books were disorganized and, to the average person, an overwhelming mess. Jake, however, was not discouraged or overwhelmed and brought order to the whole mess.

At supper time, he took a break. He found Sylvia and told her he'd be back later tonight. As an afterthought he said, "I don't like what I'm seeing. We really ought to see Milt Power's books also. I know we can't just do that without permission from the heirs, but let's just go over there first thing in the morning, just look around and take our chances."

Jake spent the rest of the night going over the accounts. At midnight he woke Sylvia up telling her some good news and some bad. The good news was that her net worth, without any consideration of the ranch's value, just stocks, bonds and investment accounts, put her current worth at about 11 million dollars.

"Wow!" she said expressing her pleasure, "Carson was really taking good care of me."

Jake replied, "Yeah, right. He was also taking good care of himself, along with the brokerage firm who were over-charging for their transactions. He's been tapping the till, long before and even when your father was still alive. In more recent times he'd been helping himself to larger sums. Can't tell you how much as those records are gone. I can get them from the investment company, but I need to collect ac-count numbers and dates. We will also likely have to make a trip to their office as soon as possible. I have an accurate balance for the ranch accounts and your personal accounts. I suggest you move everything to my dad's firm in Chicago. I also need to work on the books some more. The money just disappears and I need to find out how and where."

CHAPTER 8

THE NEXT MORNING THEY WENT TO THE POWERS LAZY 6 Ranch. The two cowboys that worked there were just lounging around at the barn. "Hey, it's good to see someone alive around here! What's going on? We've haven't been paid in a while and we are running out of food."

Sylvia told them she was sorry that they had been left to their own devices for so long and without being more fully informed.

One of them replied, "Well, we learned some of what's going on from the Sheriff's people."

Sylvia said, "We are checking on some things and Mildred's two sons are expected sometime on Friday, so look for them. You can ask them then what they want you to do for now at that time. And then they can pay you."

Inside the ranch house Jake looked over the books and general financial situation. It appeared that the Powers were just barely keeping their heads above water. There were a couple of items of note. It appears that Carson Smith had given or loaned Milt several thousand dollars here and there over the last year. Jake had noticed that item in Carson's checkbook. But it was not noted to whom or why. The other was that Mildred had withdrawn $4,000 from her private account a few days before the disastrous camping trip. There was a little cash in the desk and they decided to give some of it to the two cowboys for food.

"While we are here, let's check out what is in the headquarters in case the sons, Tom and Bob, look for us to make them an offer," Jake said. There wasn't much of anything in the house that reached beyond standard value. Maybe the old and ornate desk and one chest of drawers might have some value. Outside was Milt's old pickup truck, a few farm items and the usual miscellaneous stuff found normally on a ranch.

As they were looking about the yard, one of the cowboys said, "Whatcha looking for?"

Jake's slow response was "Oh! We always do this so people can ask what we're doing."

The cowboy just looked confused.

At that Sylvia thought, "Boy, he's not the brightest candle in the church."

Jake summed it all up with, "All we need now is a trip to the courthouse to find out how much of the ranch they actually owned and if there are any liens against it. The rest is probably leased, state trust land. As far as the cattle and horses, they can just be sold, but I'll ask Clem what he thinks. There may be some livestock that we could use. Let's face it. The only person their ranch would have any value to is you, Sylvia. And we're looking at maybe $400,000, assuming Milt owns the wells."

"We'll see what Tom and Bob want for it, but I'm sure they don't have a clue about anything and it will likely take some time. So for now, I'm accepting your job offer, mostly because I'm so curious about how all this plays out. So, as I understand it, I'm the ranch manager three days a week at the ranch manager's salary and cowboy 2 ½ days a week under Clem's direction drawing cowboy wages."

Sylvia said, "Right. Do you see any conflict or problem there?"

"No." He replied, "We can always draw straws to settle matters."

The next few days were spent setting up and getting Jake in control of things. He and Clem rode two mornings on the Power Ranch. They checked cattle, water wells and some fences and found nothing out of the ordinary. There was only a small amount of neglect here and there.

CHAPTER 9

THAT EVENING JAKE ASKED CASSIE "SINCE YOU'VE GOT JOAN feeling better, do you think she'd mind going to the drop off site? And I wouldn't mind looking for photographer Lois' camera. She said she left it behind."

"This Lois is a very suspect character in my mind. She shows up totally unexpected by anyone and leaves without any explanation. Bang! Just gone. She's got some serious explaining to do if the Sheriff ever catches up with her."

Cassie felt the trip would be good and wanted to leave early the next morning.

Jake packed up everything they might need into his four wheel drive truck that night, taking along whatever maps he could find of the area. Even though he'd been at the C-Bar ranch for four years, he had only ridden at the

Lazy 6 on the twice-annual round ups. He had always been accompanied by other cowboys and cowgirls who knew the area far better than he. So he just followed along, enjoying the round up, but not paying too much attention to where they were.

From what Joan had told them, they were dropped off at well No. 1. They were to hike straight West at 270 degrees, crossing onto the C-Bar Ranch. Eventually, they would come to a worn ranch road and, upon coming to the road, they would turn left and follow the road to the C-Bar Ranch.

After a hardy breakfast with Clem and his wife, Cassie, Jake and Joan set off, taking the road leading out from the Lazy 6. Having air conditioning in his truck gave the three adventurers great relief as even in the early morning the day was warming quickly.

The road really wasn't much of a road; it was two tracks filled with large rocks. Jake sometimes had to stop and roll a large rock out of the way. There was a lot of climbing up hills and sliding down the other side, then maybe even into a wash. The narrow two tracks allowed mesquite, prickly pear and cholla to scratch the sides of Jake's truck.

Eventually, they arrived at well No. 1. The wind mill was not turning and the stock tank was almost empty, so they got out to stretch their legs and Jake started the mill. Soon water flowed and began to fill the tank. "Think we'll leave it run for now and we'll shut it off later. It doesn't seem to be filling very fast."

Joan was walking around giving the well site a quizzi-cal look. Joan said, "This isn't where we got dropped off," she said. "Where we started had a small board corral next to the stock tank."

"Guess we will continue to water well No. 2," Jake suggested. After another hour of slow driving over even rougher road and according to the map, they came to water well No. 2. Joan recognized the place right away. "Yes, this is it!" she exclaimed. "There is the corral. We started here."

Jake decided to try his cell phone and it worked. Calling Clem he told him where they were and that the hiking party was apparently dropped off at a different location. From what he could see from the map, if they followed their instructions of following the compass due west, they would miss the C-Bar Ranch road by a very long way and walk into a very bare, desolate area with many, many miles of wasteland to cross before coming to anything.

Clem took all this in in wonderment. Jake added they were going to try and find the campsite and then head home. He added, "I had to start two windmills as the tanks were about empty. Those two alleged cowboys, Slick and Slouch, hadn't been doing diddly squat. Maybe you can inspire them to check the other wells." "Will do," Clem answered.

Taking a lunch break it was decided to try to find the campsite. After one hour of traveling just a path, they just about gave up on going any further. When Joan said, "It was in a big clump of trees that you see along river and creek banks. Only this was a dry creek bed." As they were almost to a spot that appeared open that could be a dry creek bed, they plowed ahead and did come to a dry creek bed.

Jake noted the GPS coordinates and stated they could come back here another time. Joan again told them about the mysterious Lois wanting to go back the way they had come, considering Mildred's seemingly failing condition.

At the well where they had been dropped off there was cell phone service, weak as it was, and there was water.

Lois had told Jake that at the time Milt and Carson wanted to continue on. They said they wanted to see and understand more about this vast land they managed. Feeling they were close to the road to go back on and had come this far, why not continue? The women, however, were pretty much done for. Neither of them had spent any time on the ranch's spreading land, only at ranch headquarters and hearing from the cowboys what all they knew about the land. So the group split up thinking they were coming close to the C-Bar Ranch headquarters, or at best stronger cell phone service.

Jake and his group had turned around and pretty much followed the route that they had come by. After an hour Cassie cried out, "What's that over there?" Jake looked at what appeared to be Lois' black camera bag. Stopping, he picked it up, anxiously wanting to see what was inside. However, coolness of his mind prevailed. "Maybe it's best to leave it untouched. Finger prints and such. We'll let Sheriff Rogers figure this out."

They headed back and the rest of the trip was uneventful.

The Sheriff showed up later that evening to collect the camera bag. At this time he confided in them, "It looks like Mildred's medications had been tampered with. She was very short on insulin and showed high levels of heavy metals in her system. Preliminary tests showed her capsules of Vitamin D had been emptied and replaced with powdered mercury. Unfortunately, no fingerprints or other traceable evidence were found. The camera, however, is a real windfall."

"Lois, the mysterious photographer, was the most likely person to have shot Milt Powers and Carson Smith, even though Joan said she never left them and that the distance between the murder scene and where the women were at any time was a considerable distance. That leaves the ATV driver who dropped them off at a different location. He was the most likely suspect to have the opportunity and it also seems to me a third party may be involved."

CHAPTER 10

THE FOLLOWING WEEK ARRIVED. EVERYONE WAS SOMEwhat on edge and curious about the arrival of Milt and Mildred's sons, Tom and Bob. What might they be planning? About 11:00 AM they arrived in a cloud of dust at the Lazy 6, driving two rented midsize cars.

Sylvia had sent Juanita to clean up a bit and to have some refreshments ready. They seemed happy and jovial as Juanita greeted them and invited them inside. Both families were dressed in new boots, western shirts and hats. They were dressed to the Western 9's.

As they proceeded towards the house, they were waylaid by the two cowboys, who immediately announced they hadn't paid in three weeks. They wanted to be paid today and added that they wanted to be kept on the payroll.

Tom said, "Well, we just got here and need to see what's going on. We'll settle up with you both this afternoon."

One of the cowboys said, "OK, but don't forget you said this afternoon."

The other cowboy angrily said, "We are getting tired of working for free." And with that, the two retreated to their lounge chairs outside the tack room.

Juanita called the C-Bar and told Sylvia that Tom and Bob had arrived. Sylvia said she would collect Jake and be right over. Upon their arrival, they made small talk and exchanged pleasantries. Tom told them that when settling down to business, the two cowboys wanted to be paid and they needed to decide what to do with them. Jake suggested they look at their parents' checkbook and see how much money they made and when they were paid last. As a result of Jake and Sylvia snooping around, they already knew.

But Tom and Bob did look and found there wasn't much cash in the checkbook or the bank for that matter. Tom, looking for some advice said, "What would you do?"

After a little thought Jake said, "Pay them off and fire them. They aren't worth a crap. We can cover the Lazy 6 needs with our crew for a short time. We'd better have Clem, our foreman, come over and help you with this. And we'll have him stay until these two yahoos pack up and leave."

"Bob," Tom suggested, "How about you going down there and ask them how much we owe them."

Bob proceeded down to the tack room finding the two cowboys still relaxing in their lounge chairs that they had left them in. They told him what they were due adding that they weren't asking anything for all the extra work they had done or for purchases that they had made for food. Bob agreed and went back to the house reporting what they had said.

Jake smiled, "Looks like they gave themselves a nice pay raise and an extra week of work." He suggested that they wait until Clem arrived. Clem and the two boys could then go down together and pay them off and fire them. Then Clem and one of the boys would stay with them to make sure they didn't run off with things that weren't theirs. The pay and firing drew loud protests from the two now former employees, who now claimed that everything in sight belonged to them. Clem kept them going with junk that would fill the boy's pickup truck so they couldn't take anything of value.

The real contest came over the saddles. One claimed Milt's fine saddle was his. And Clem asked, "How come Milt always rode in it?"

"I let him," was the cowboys defiant answer.

"How come he rode in it long before you ever started doing nothing here on the Lazy 6."

"Well, it's mine."

Clem said, "OK, take all your grievances to one of those lawyer type fellas in town. He'll get you what you deserve;

a big-ass bill. Don't come back here either. If you show up in the dark of night prowling around, this Colt 45 won't be on my hip. It'll be in my hand." Clem was a man to be taken very seriously and they knew that. So they left shouting insults and went raising a big cloud of dust.

"Damn!" Bob said to Clem. "That was just like something out of the Old West."

Clem squinted his eyes and said, "The Old West never left."

They had lunch on the mesquite and palo verde shaded patio of the ranch house.

The enchiladas and tacos were consumed by the boys and their family with lots of enthusiasm and were washed down with several bottles of Corona Beer. The boys again mentioned they were interested in selling the ranch. Jake suggested they look around and get an idea of what was there and what the market value might be.

"Well," Tom began. "Our folks had always done very well here and they supported a thousand head of cattle on almost two hundred thousand acres. We're sure the value is evident. Even in just the land itself, we're looking at least two million dollars. The cattle, horses and equipment would be another million. So we are probably looking at about three million dollars for the whole outfit, lock, stock and barrel."

Jake and Sylvia just looked serious as if carefully considering their expectations. Jake, after a few minutes of silence, unfortunately, shattered their dreams by stating that their parents didn't own the land.

"It's state trust land and was leased by your parents. The lease was up this year. Do you have the money to lease it back?" Jake inquired. "Your father was negotiating with Carson for money for the lease." Not to add insult to injury he told them that he doubted there were a thousand head of cattle as the last round up only yielded 400 head, some of which were sold.

They concluded with Jake saying that tomorrow they should take time to make arrangements for their parents. Then take the rest of Saturday and Sunday and look around and size up things. And then on Monday visit the court-house, the bank and maybe a realtor. They would regroup on Wednesday to see where they were at on things. In the meantime, Juanita would be at their disposal at the house doing housekeeping and cooking. Clem and his crew would look after the ranch work.

With everyone else going their own ways, Clem and Jake headed to their trucks.

At that point Clem announced, "Jake, I hired a new cow-boy and he'll start with us on Monday. He'll, in part, fill in for your absence, not that you were much of a hand in the first place," he said gruffly. "Old Wild Bill is his handle. He's a top hand. Now that those two idiots at the Lazy 6 finally got sent down the road, we might need another hand as Milt's two boys are in over their heads."

"I expect the Princess will buy them out for a whole lot less than what you guys may think. So, with that, we might consider rounding up all of the cattle and bring Nate Bloom, the cattle buyer in whom often buys direct at round ups. I want to sort the cattle as there are some really good ones there. With Nate buying on the spot, the two boys will be excited about getting a check right away. What do you think?"

"You are the boss, Clem."

"You're the manager, Jake. What do you want to do, draw straws?"

With that Jake headed to his trailer just to take a long nap and enjoy some peace and quiet. "What happened to my quiet and relaxed lifestyle I enjoyed so much?"

Cassie was an unexpected but very pleasant addition to his life. How long have I known her now? He thought about it. Two weeks maybe. I've not treated her as well as I could have and at that deep sleep engulfed him. He awoke in the middle of the night and rolled over to find Cassie there. He kissed her and held her close.

CHAPTER 11

AFTER BREAKFAST THE NEXT MORNING, CASSIE WENT TO look after Joan. Jake went to what was now his office at Sylvia's main house. He again looked at Milt's records and those that had been made at the last several round-ups. He had noted that Sylvia's name did not appear on any of the brokerage documents, just Carson Smith's and her father's. He recognized that they only had two days, Monday and Tuesday, to look into the investment and brokerage firm in Tucson. A trip to the bank to see who could sign checks was in order and then to the county records office to see who had ownership of the ranch.

Jake then called the brokerage company in Tucson to make an appointment with them at one o'clock that afternoon. He informed them that their intention was to take

Carson Smith and Sylvia's father's name off of the documents. And at that time Jake asked the brokerage company not to do anything with either the funds or accounts until they got there and changed the names.

Jake was dumbfounded to find Sylvia's name not on anything, just her father's and Carson Smith's. They had brought Smith's death certificate, but that wasn't enough. And Sylvia didn't have the authority to put Jake in charge. Jake really wasn't dressed right for the occasion either. Western shirt, faded jeans, scruffy boots, but he had not expected this problem. He just smiled at the three brokers as this was a major account for them. Their two senior officers had joined them.

"Well, we want to resolve this quickly, so I'll contact a local attorney to wrap this up as I am sure you are aware of Sylvia's obvious legal right to these accounts which are remarkably still in her father's name." said Jake. "We are still requesting that you take no action or transfers."

They acted like he and Sylvia were totally naive about investments. He'd fix that problem as soon as he could. For now, he closed the accounts that funneled money into Carson's personal accounts. There were also two other accounts that didn't seem quite right to him and favored the brokerage company by charging one and a half per cent to move investments from one place to another. The brokerage firm protested aggressively saying that this was not how Robert Simmons made so much money on his investments.

"I'm sure you know what you're doing," Jake politely responded. "But let's say you have $100,000 to invest for me. Show me how much you had made for me in the time that we next meet, I'll show you what I would have made. I know what you think, that I'm just a dumb ass cowboy, but it's all a matter of results."

With that the brokerage people decided that, until all matters were clarified and settled, they would wait. They were hoping to gain a positive relationship with these two clients, whom, as Jake suspected, felt that he and Sylvia knew very little about finances.

As they left, Jake called his father's long-time attorney in Chicago seeking a reference for a legal firm in Tucson to help them gain control of all the investments currently in the hands of the Tucson brokerage. The attorney ultimately recommended a firm in Tucson that they had worked with before. The Chicago attorney also said he would call the selected firm ahead of time to tell them that Jake and Sylvia were on their way over. Hopefully, they could be seen right away.

It was definitely a high class and likely a pricey adventure. The attorneys quickly assessed what needed to be done and upon Jake's insistence, acted very quickly. Jake paid the retainer without question from his own resources. He wanted Sylvia's funds available for the potential purchase of the Lazy 6 Ranch.

Driving back with Sylvia, Jake was in a hostile mood. Sylvia said to Jake, "You must not be too uninformed about the stock market, if that information I pulled up on you showed you were worth $2.5 million."

"I'm not bragging or trying to impress you, Sylvia, but that number is like $3 million now. And I didn't even work on it very much. I really don't need anything more. You pay me well for what I want to do. A 24 foot travel trailer is like a luxury home for me. My old truck runs just fine and my boss, Clem, leaves me alone. I even enjoy the fact that he is so grouchy."

"Now there is a new person in my life. I don't know what she sees in me and she knows nothing about my background."

"I do," Sylvia said. "Believe me, Jake, it is not money. I have made so many mistakes in my life, it hurts. You're likely the biggest. Now we have three murders to deal with. I can't rest without answers."

They rode the rest of the way home in silence.

Two days later his Tucson attorneys called stating that everything had been taken care of. They only had to go back to the brokerage company and sign a few papers. One of the senior attorneys would go with them. Jake liked the sound of that. He wanted to humble those yahoos who thought they knew everything.

The signing went smoothly at the brokerage. The brokers now knew what kind of people they were up against. Formalities had been taken care of and Jake and Sylvia were now in charge of all the funds. Jake at this time announced that all funds, accounts, etc. are being transferred to French & Son in Chicago. The dismay and disappointment of the brokerage people was evident. "French & Son that pompous, high society outfit is not in your league. We will take care of you first class."

"Sure," Jake responded. "You tried to make a sizable change in our accounts when you were asked not to do anything right now."

The brokerage people responded by telling him that that didn't happen. They were looking out for his best interest, better than that French & Son outfit could. He'd be forgotten in a week.

Jake cast his eyes over all of them with his attorney trying to keep a straight face. "French & Son," he said, "I know they won't forget me. I'm the son."

The local bank, upon presentation of the death certificates, had no trouble signing the bank assets to Sylvia as the owner and Jake as ranch manager, Sylvia maintaining her private accounts on her own. The property and assessor office put the property in Sylvia's name, but only after receiving some documents from the Tucson lawyer.

CHAPTER 12

W ITH ALL THE FINANCIAL STUFF BEHIND THEM, THEY could now deal with Tom and Bob Powers. At this time, however, they were unsure about everything, not knowing what the two brothers wanted to do. They also needed to find out what Clem had found in the way of ranch conditions.

Clem, Sylvia and Jake agreed to meet later that night. Clem's report was not unfavorable. The ranch equipment was in a questionable state of repair. The buildings were in great condition. All five wells were working, but the underground water levels had become lower than expected. The fences in many places needed extensive repairs. Jake reported that only ten acres were deeded to the Powers family. These ten acres consisted of the headquarters house and buildings and also just one well.

Mid Wednesday morning they all sat down together. The boys felt their ranch was worth at least $1 million. So they placed a value on numerous items. Jake countered their evaluations with both sides compromising and agreeing in principle. They took a break for a lunch that Juanita had prepared. Back at it again in the afternoon, they became stalemated. The boys still held a much higher view of the value to the land.

Jake considering what to do asked them, "What do you want to do at this time?"

Tom indicated he wanted $750,000 for the ranch itself and the sale of cattle at current market rate.

Jake said, "We are offering $300,000 in cash for everything."

Tom and Bob said almost in unison, "Can't do it!"

Jake replied, "We really appreciate your time with us and we appreciate your consideration of us as buyers. We'll continue to work the ranch until this time next week at which time you'll be on your own. You need to apply to lease the land again and be prepared to pay for it upon acceptance. You will also need a couple of hired hands to keep things going. From our experience with the last two, you might have an idea that this could be a challenge, especially with absentee owners, so thank you again for your time."

With that he rose to leave with Clem following. Sylvia was struck dumbfounded. She didn't know what to say or do. She realized she couldn't do anything without Jake's approval. She just didn't have that much cash money. What was Jake thinking? As she was leaving, she saw Clem closing the ranch driveway gate. He stopped and reopened it for her to drive through. Stopping she asked, "What in the world is Jake thinking about now?"

Clem sort of stared off into the mountains and quietly replied, "Well, he's already applied to lease the ranch next year. Only one of the five wells is owned by the Powers family. That gives the lease four wells. We don't need the ranch house, buildings or corrals. So, Jake figures we might get what we want for free. And it looks to me like he just saved you $1 million."

CHAPTER 13

ON THIS MONDAY, WHILE JAKE AND SYLVIA WERE TRYING to solve financial problems, Clem was expecting his new hire, Ol' Wild Bill, to show up. He thought he might show up at the Lazy Six and felt he should drop a note off as to where they should meet. Upon arriving at the Lazy Six, he found a battered old pick up that couldn't be anybody but Bill's parked at the bunk house. Searching about, no sign of Ol' Wild Bill's presence was found, except one of the better horses was missing. Clem thought, "Looks like Bill is already checking things out."

Ol' Wild Bill wasn't a spring chicken but he was lean and hard. The straw hat he wore was old and battered, held together by sweat, dirt and cow manure. His younger days had been spent breaking horses, showing them and tending cattle for people who really didn't know what they were doing. But his performance and abilities gained their total confidence in him. In time with ownership changes and age comes, so Ol' Will Bill decided to semi retire to a steadier job situation that of helping out ranches with their basic livestock and facility needs.

It also appeared that Bill had moved his things into the bunk house and straightened a bit. Sure is my kind of a guy was Clem's thought. He left a note on the bunk house door to come to the C-Bar Ranch when he got back.

Ol' Wild Bill showed up at the C-Bar about noon just in time, for a well prepared lunch being served for Clem, Cassie, Bob Bissell, Clay Robertson and Joan. After introductions and small talk, lunch was consumed. Clem, Bob, Bill and Clay retired to the ranch foreman's tree shaded patio. Clem explained about the delicate situation they were in, with the three recent deaths and the Lazy Six owner's undecided about what they wanted to do. He added that no matter what happens this was going to be a secure job for all of them. He then explained that Bob Bissell would come over on Tuesday and Wednesday to work with Ol' Wild Bill. Then on Thursday and Friday Clay Robertson would be over.

Jake got home late that Monday evening only to find Cassie not there yet. "Must be off doing some girl things," he thought and he turned in early. Awakening at 3 am he realized he was alone. He looked around more observantly, discovering that most of her things were gone, too. He realized quickly that she had left him and suddenly realized how much he had grown to care for her and how empty the trailer seemed without her.

He got into his truck and drove to the Stop and Go. It was closed and her truck wasn't in sight. He went on further and passed her old apartment, not finding her truck there either, nor any sign of anyone living there. He tried calling her on the cell phone. Still there was no answer. Going home was the only thing he could do. First thing in the morning, he would find Joan to find out what she might know.

At 7 am. Jake was knocking on Joan's door. "C'mon in!" she said. "I was expecting you and I have some coffee ready. Boy! You have really been busy. So much has been going on. What's happening with the Powers boys?" she queried as she poured coffee into a thick, heavy mug.

"Where is Cassie?" he inquired meekly.

"Well, Jake, she has been helping me more than you know. I miss her already and have really gotten to feel close to her. It's not my place to say but you haven't treated her very well. Like most guys, just taking her for granted."

"Oh no! I'm not like that. I'll make it up to her. Maybe I could buy her a new pickup truck."

"Jake, you probably couldn't afford one and that's not the most romantic thing I ever heard of. You're a really nice guy, but when it comes to women, you're as dumb as a box

of rocks. Cassie is a really nice girl. She has quit here and
was able to get her job back at the Stop N Go. I suspect a lot
of this has to do with all the time you've been spending with
Sylvia."

"Do I have a choice, Joan? She's my boss and has more
problems and situations that I can hardly keep up with."

"Well, I hope you find her and have a long talk with her
and bring her back for me, but mostly for you. I'm warning
you, Jake, don't trust Sylvia for a moment. She's bad news.
So good luck and let me know as soon as you can how you
did with her."

Walking back to his trailer, he called Cassie on the cell
phone. After many rings, she answered. All he could say,
choked up as he had become, was, "I'm so sorry, Cassie."

Her answer was silence.

"I want to see you right away."

"Oh." was her clipped reply.

"I'll come to you right away," Jake pleaded.

"I don't want you to see where I am."

"OK. Where should we meet then?"

Cassie said, "You tell me. You're the one who called."

"How about at my place?"

"I guess."

"Can you come now?"

"I'll be there sometime this morning," she said.

"Good," Jake said relieved, "I'll be waiting."

"Wow!" Jake thought. "She is sure wound up about something." He went home, cleaned himself up, shaved and straightened up the trailer and paced around anxiously trying to think about what to do and say.

It was almost eleven when Cassie drove up and walked in. He took her in his arms and held her feeling somewhat awkward. She sat down and he offered her something to drink. "Some of that coffee would be OK," she replied.

Jake said, "I don't know where to start. I thought you were moving in here."

She replied with, "You never asked me."

"But I did."

Her answer to that was, "That invite sounded more like you were looking for someone to fan the blankets with."

He said, "Cassie, you don't know how much you mean to me."

"You never told me," was her answer.

"Guess with getting too preoccupied with the state of affairs, I took everything for granted," he said.

"Everything or just me?" she replied. And so the morning went. The noon hour passed and in the early afternoon the subject of Sylvia came up. Cassie stated, "I told you she was evil and every time I turn around you're running off some place with her. I won't and will not play second fiddle to her. If you want me, you're going to have to do something about her. Not second, third or last. Now! I gotta go or I'll be late for work."

"Can I pick you up after work?" Jake asked.

"No."

"Let's talk some more about this later. I love you, Cassie."

"I love you, too, Jake." And she was gone. Her truck rumbled out in a cloud of dust.

Jake could not believe how well he could screw things up with people he never realized meant so much to him. He put a lot on the back burner. And decided that when it came to push came to shove, all he really wanted was a very quiet life with her. The problem was three unsolved murders, responsibility to some people who he really didn't feel obligated to and he felt more unsure as to who these people actually were. He sincerely felt that if he couldn't get his act together with Cassie, he couldn't resolve anything else.

He talked to Clem about all of this and Clem offered part of the solution.

"Why don't we hire Cassie as a ranch hand, so that she won't feel we are just giving her some kind of token job? She's very good at riding but needs lots of work on roping. You might talk to Joan about making the Smith place headquarters for both ranches. My wife could use some help trying to feed the hungriest cowboys you could find to hire. Anyway, we could try her out, if you're wanting to. That way we could gain a hand that we could all use. What do you think, Jake?"

Jake's answer was, "Let's just draw straws."

When Cassie arrived late that morning, she was subdued. Jake started off with his thoughts of wishing they could just run off and disappear, but followed then with addressing the challenge that was in front of them.

First, he expressed his ultimate, total desire to be just with her. Not waiting for a response from her, he then reviewed Clem's desire to hire her as a ranch hand besides spending time with Joan also and developing the Carson place into a headquarters. He also mentioned the possibility of moving to the Powers Ranch, if the boys decided to sell, thereby creating a further distance from Sylvia's presence. The Powers Ranch house, which held a considerably western appeal, would be desirable. But here again, it depended on the two sons' decisions. In the meantime, they would use the 24 foot travel trailer Jake felt most at home there.

"I want to do this, Jake. I love you but sometimes things seem so complex."

Jake replied, "They are for now, but together we need to enjoy and appreciate who we are. As you can see, I'm putting the Princess out to pasture. But she is still the boss and the owner of the ranch. So for now, it's the trailer and this hammock."

"OK," Cassie responded. "I'm not ever playing second fiddle to anyone. Remember that. I did think you would come around and brought all of my things along with me.

Not that this is the biggest place I ever lived, but I assume I'm in charge of where things are going to be put."

"Yes, you are and then some. Want to go to the Show Me Later? Or perhaps I can grill something."

"Yes, please. Grill something and start a fire in the fire pit. I'll pop a bottle of Pinot Noir which I brought."

Jake, relaxing in the hammock said, "Damn, I'll never take this for granted."

CHAPTER 14

ARLY THE NEXT MORNING, BOB, CLAY AND JAKE DROVE over to Sylvia's house. Cassie headed over to Joan's house to clear space in what had been Carson Smith's office. Juanita told the boys that Sylvia was not there as she had gone on one of her trips.

Jake explained that they were moving the office to Carson's old office to centralize activities and not disturb Sylvia's privacy. The three of them easily loaded everything into Jake's pickup and drove to Joan's house.

Revitalization of Carson's old office found Joan very enthusiastic about the new setup as Carson spent most of his time in the office. Even though Jake was only going to be there part of the time, it would not seem as lonely.

CHAPTER 15

THE DATE FOR THE LEASE RENEWAL CAME AND WENT. TOM and Bob Powers made no effort to renew, so Jake's option was accepted by the State Trust land office. Another three weeks passed without hearing from Tom or Bob. Jake then called the two brothers asking who was looking after things and also told them that their lease had run out. They would need to round up their cattle to sell or the new lessee/owner could claim them.

Jake then offered to arrange a round up in three or four weeks. Then he offered to buy the buildings, ten acres of land and the one well for $200,000 cash. All they needed to do was clear out the house of personal items and be there representing the family at the round up.

Tom reluctantly agreed saying that he and Bob would be out a couple of days before the roundup.

CHAPTER 16

C LEM WAS WORKING CASSIE TO DEATH RIDING RANGE with various cowboys and learning the ranch in detail. Clem was impressed with Cassie's abilities and had her doing more leadership roles. Those who worked with her didn't seem to mind. Things got done and that was the long and the short of it. They all also recognized that she and Joan could really cook. They all seemed to be happy with the way things were going.

The management arrangement was that Jake was in charge Monday through Wednesday of the overall management and rode under Clem's direction as a cowboy on Thursdays, Fridays and a half day on Saturday. For some strange reason this really worked well, mostly because it paralleled the past arrangement between Carson Smith and

Clem. In the past, Clem managed the day-to-day activities, while Carson would take care of the books and bills. The difference now was everybody knew what was going on and they weren't hesitant to ask questions and offer suggestions. Jake, however, mostly savored his days of cowboying.

The roundup was still a couple of weeks off and the Powers brothers, now had agreed to sell for the suggested price with some negotiating options. Jake and Clem then decided to look the Lazy 6 over a little more closely.

Ol' Wild Bill and Cassie were assigned to check the condition of perimeter fences very closely. While making their rounds, they were in a remote area, when Bill stopped suddenly and looked. He called to Cassie, "Something doesn't look right over there." He pointed to an area of dense palo verdes, mesquite, ironwood, cactus and plenty of undergrowth.

Cassie rode over exclaiming, "What's so strange about that!"

"Looks like a place to hide something," said Ol' Wild Bill. "And it hasn't been very well maintained either. We'd better check it out and be very careful at that."

They rode over and shortly discovered a barely discernible path leading into the thicket. Bill dismounted and Cassie held his horse. Following the path, he came upon a small holding pen with four steers in it. They looked to be about 500 pounds or maybe a little better. The pen had hay and water in it. The pen looked like it had been there for a long time and the steers appeared to be ready for someone to pick them up in the next night or two.

Bill climbed from the thicket and told Cassie of his findings. "We'd better head back right away as those steers appear to be ready for pick up."

They rode straight back to the C-Bar headquarters and found Clem in the barn. There they reported their findings. Clem said he felt that for some time something like that might be going on as roundups continually came up a little short each time. The only thing to do now was to call Sheriff Rogers.

Rogers was very interested in this development and said, "You people out on the C-Bar Ranch are really keeping things hopping. Maybe we should move the Sheriff's office out to the ranch to save time and gas money." Then he said from the serious side of things, "Probably there was some sort of vehicle access to the pen from the adjacent property." He would immediately send out Deputy Tom Hickman to stake the site out, even if it took all night.

When Deputy Hickman arrived, Clem and Ol' Wild Bill went with him. They did find a barely discernible two track path on the adjacent property that lead to the pen containing the four steers.

After some discussion among the three men, Deputy Hickman said he would stay back in the area for the evening and Clem and Ol' Wild Bill returned to the ranch. He found a well-hidden place in which he could hide and watch for developments. He had come in his own personal car hoping to draw less attention than a marked patrol car would, should he be seen. His thermos of coffee was full and his wife, Rebekah, had made him three ham and cheese sandwiches.

He didn't have to wait very long. At about 10 PM an older model pickup truck pulling a fourteen foot stock trailer came very slowly with its lights out past Hickman's hidden observation post. It appeared to be occupied by only one person.

The trailer was backed down to the hidden pen. The gates were opened and the steers easily loaded after catching the aroma of alfalfa hay. Gates snapped closed and the truck pulled silently out, again with lights off. The truck and trailer pulled out in a different direction from which it came in across the desert. Deputy Hickman knew it would eventually come out on Rt. 287. He followed at a great distance, so as not to alarm the now apparent rustler.

They traveled to Rt. 287, where the pickup driver turned on his lights, and went onto the highway. Deputy Hickman was unsure whether the rustler had turned right or left. But he reasoned that the rustler would go left to pick up the nearby I-10. He soon caught up with the rustler. Here again, he didn't want to follow too closely and he let a couple of cars get in between them. He could now see that the pickup truck and trailer were distantly in sight. They turned into the east bound lane on I-10 heading to New Mexico.

At a truck stop they pulled in and the driver went into the restaurant to place an order. Tom now sprang into action attaching a tracking device to the bottom of the truck. He called into the office dispatcher to update them on what was going on and asking what to do. He was advised to continue to follow the truck, but not to do anything as he wasn't in his county of jurisdiction or even Arizona for that matter. Tom stayed out of sight and when the truck driver came out, he followed at a distance, as his tracking device kept him accurately informed if he should lose him.

After another fifty miles, the rustler turned off and made a series of turns through a small town. Tom, noting all of this, broke off his following and headed for home. He turned all of this information over to the Sheriff and said that the tracking device on the truck should lead to where the rustler lived. Wayne Rogers contacted the local authorities in New Mexico, giving them the general directions to where he thought the cattle might have been dropped off.

The local authorities did acknowledge that there was a cattle trader in the area and that they would check it out, looking for the four steers with a Lazy 6 brand. The tracking device did find where the truck stopped the next day. No surprise there as it was the house of the two former Lazy 6 cowboys, both of whom were taken into custody with their usual complaints of mistreatment and unfairness.

Further investigation found they were related to the cattle trader in New Mexico. Checking at the local cattle auction they found the rustlers had sold cattle there for many years, likely rebranding the Lazy 6 brand with the Double O brand. The brand inspector was called in and it was found how easy it was to alter the Lazy 6 brand to the Double O. They would fatten up the stolen stock some and let the rebrand age some. The cattle dealer was arrested also.

The rustlers were unable to post bond and ended up living in the county's accommodations while awaiting trial.

CHAPTER 17

THIS WAS NOT A GOOD TIME FOR THIS TO HAPPEN. CASSIE'S old pickup truck died and could not be restarted. That and the four bald tires didn't invite rescue for the faded brown Datsun. Its demise was a sorrow for Cassie. She'd had the truck since high school and this was like losing a close relative. Jake suggested that they go to Tucson to a dealer and find a replacement.

Cassie said, "My truck isn't worth anything. And I've only got maybe $400 in cash."

Jake looked at her and stated, "We're in this together. Get all of your stuff out of your truck and we'll go to Tucson first thing in the morning. I'll get Bob and Clay to get rid of your old truck. So don't expect it to be here when we come back."

She looked at him speculating. Jake said, "So, let me clear this with Clem and tell Bob and Clay what I want them to do."

The trip to Tucson was uneventful and they mostly talked about events at the ranch. When they arrived at the dealership, Cassie told Jake she only had actually $378.

He answered, "When money comes up, you let me do the talking."

The salesman surprised Cassie when he greeted them by their names and acted as if he was expecting them. Then escorted them to five pickups, brand new and parked in a row. "Look them over, Cassie," Jake said. "Sorry but we are ranch people, so it has to be a four wheel drive, three quarter ton, big V-8 engine pickup."

With tears streaming from her eyes, she said, "I can't begin to even make payments on something like this."

The salesman pulled her aside and said, "He's paying cash, Miss. He called yesterday for us to do a credit check and arranged it."

Cassie couldn't come to grips with this. Just stared and looked in disbelief. She was unable to follow the discussion Jake and the salesman were having over the merits of the different trucks. Finally, Jake told the salesman they would take one of the trucks, but he wanted to take Cassie to lunch and get her settled down.

The restaurant was quiet and the waitress offered them a table in a private room. Jake then explained some about his wealth coming from investments he made while working for his father. The mention of his father took Cassie by surprise. It had never crossed her mind about his having parents.

"I don't think I can do this today," she told him.

Jake replied, "It's too late, Cassie. Clay and Bob have junked your Datsun while we were here. So, tell you what. They are all good trucks and the costs mean nothing to me. Just pick out one of the color you like best."

Upon their return to the dealership, Cassie was only somewhat more composed but did select a bronze colored truck. She took the title and related paperwork in silence. Her tears were flowing. The title was in her name, the receipt paid-in-full. Cassie couldn't come to grips with all of this. So Jake drove the new truck with Cassie beside him struggling with her emotions. Jake told the salesman he would have two ranch hands pick up his truck tomorrow.

CHAPTER 18

JAKE DIDN'T TALK TO HIS FATHER VERY OFTEN. HE STILL FELT he was disappointed and disapproving of Jake's decision to leave the firm. So his father's call one Sunday was a great surprise. His father sounded weak and was far from his usual take charge and commanding demeanor.

"What's going on, dad? You don't sound like your normal self." Jake queried.

"Well son. I'm not. Had some issues last week and finally went to a doctor. You know, I haven't had a physical in years. Always felt fine, but not so now. Doctor said I need to change my lifestyle, eat better, sleep more, walk more, get outside more and get away from that computer. And also get away from all that smoke in the office. You know, I have always allowed smoking in the office as I like smoking a few cigars during the day. The doctor said my heart was in really bad shape and I might not make it till Christmas at the rate I'm going. That's about as grim as it can get. I want to come out to see you and maybe get somewhat refreshed with a change of scenery. You always seem to be upbeat and happy when I talk to you. I need some of that."

"Wow! That is something dad and we will really look forward to your visit. We have a lot of stuff going on right now and a round-up coming in a few weeks that you won't want to miss. There will be a lot of people I want you to meet, especially Cassie. You're going to see what keeps me motivated and the people you will meet will be real. No phony stuff here. Pack light. Anything you need we can pick up at local stores. Fly out real soon and we'll get you at the airport. Can't tell you how much this means to me."

Jake was so excited he found Cassie and told her about all of it. "Where are you going to put him up?" she asked with a smile. "We'll be at that mansion of a trailer you have. The Powers family will be in the Lazy 6 ranch house. Clem's family will be in for the round-up and I don't think bunking in with the cowboys would be your dad's forte. So that leaves Sylvia, heaven forbid, and Joan. Now that I think of it, Joan will be perfect. She has the time and having a guest will help her out of the doldrums. She knows everybody and where everything is. She'll really be able to look after him. Now all you need to do, Jake, is to talk her into it."

Joan was very enthusiastic about entertaining Jeff French. And set about reorganizing the guest bedroom, making sure there was plenty of space, etc. She hadn't had any guests in years and looked forward to having someone to eat lunch with on the shaded patio.

Four days later Jake received a message from his father stating he would arrive the next morning in a private Lear jet he had chartered at the local airport. He received his dad's message that the plane would land at 10:18 AM. So he and Cassie drove to the airport in Joan's car. The plane landed at exactly 10:18. The door opened and his dad stepped out telling the pilot this is where to pick him up when he would fly back to Chicago. For now, his dad lightheartedly said to the pilots, "Don't get lost flying to Dallas," which was their next stop.

After introductions and greetings, they loaded up into Joan's car.

"Can't see you driving a car, son." Jeff French observed.

"Well dad. The truck can only hold two people."

"Still got that old wreck you stole off that old man in Chicago?"

"Yeah, dad, but it runs good."

"Jake, you sure can be stubborn about things."

"I know. I'm just like my dad."

That brought a round of laughter from all of them. Cassie brought Jeff French up to date about Joan's husband being killed a month or so ago. And it was also Joan's husband that was in charge of the investments. Jake added that he had found some improprieties of his handling in Sylvia's accounts and ranch accounts. He added that he wanted his dad to look at the books as there were a few items he wasn't satisfied with.

They took Jeff to Joan's house and got past some more introductions. After some small talk, they had a light lunch and Jeff then opted for a nap. Cassie and Jake began to walk to the travel trailer, which was now their primary home.

A County Sheriff's patrol car turned in the yard with Sheriff Rogers at the wheel. Rolling down his window he said to them, "This ranch seems to have so much going on I thought I'd save myself a trip and check with you to see what's new before I go back to the office."

Jake invited him to the patio for some iced tea. Once they had settled down, Jake asked about the missing Lois and the camera and bag. Rogers said that he really didn't want to talk about all of this but was hoping something of relevance maybe uncovered soon. The Sheriff said he was really frustrated having almost nothing with which to go on; however, a camera bag was a real windfall. It was loaded with finger prints belonging to a 23 year old woman named Louisa Handbeck, no known current address, but authorities had been looking for her for a couple years now. There were several warrants out for her arrest, mostly for being some sort of a con artist and passing bad checks, along with several felony items.

"We checked the pictures she took," he said, "And she's no photographer. The pictures she took didn't add anything to our investigation, although Joan said she had never left them. This Lois is our number two suspect. Now having a murder warrant out for her added to what is already out there, she'll turn up sooner or later."

"A couple of things really bother me; however, if she slipped away at night, Smith and Powers would have been camping and likely still asleep. As it was, they were hiking and pretty far from where the three women were. I'd sure like to catch up with that ATV driver who apparently dropped them off in the wrong location. Adding to this mess is Joan's babbling 'chee nu'.

"Mildred felt someone was trying to kill her, which may be true as her medications had been tampered with. This was found upon checking her insulin and it was found to be diluted. Her blood thinner medication had also been compromised. The capsule contents had been poured out and replaced with powdered mercury. The coroner did find high levels of heavy metal in her system upon his second and more detailed autopsy."

The sheriff seemed to be at a loss about this whole situation; two men who were shot at a distant and very remote location without any probable cause or reason. Jake pressed him on his suspect list.

"Well, Jake, I do have a list."

"Lois with her disappearance, but how could she cover that much distance and be gone a long time without Joan noticing, even though her state of mind was certainly impaired."

"The unknown ATV driver certainly had the opportunity. Can't figure out where he came from and we think maybe he and Lois were in this together. However, this Lois was not around to tamper with Mildred's medications either. Could be she isn't the one, but how does she fit in on this rather sordid story? I don't know."

"Maybe Milt and Mildred's two sons might know something. Maybe they were looking for a big inheritance of some sort."

Jake was candid with the Sheriff. "With what you know now, how does the overall subject list look?"

He said, "It's still early yet and there are only a few things I can actually discuss with you; however, aside from the people I already mentioned, we're basically looking at everybody. I feel it took two or more to commit this crime and I'm sure anxious to catch up with the ATV driver and that Lois."

"And to be honest with you, Jake, you're still on the list also, as you sure found the victims quickly. You could have ridden to the cabin and just hung around until the next morning. Then you could have gone over and covered them up and rode out the next morning."

"What was the motive? I don't have a clue. And who it might be? I keep wondering about those two so-called cowboys at the Lazy 6. Maybe they thought the two sons might keep the place and let them run it. There was also the time frame in which in which no one can alibi for them. Bob and Clay are in the same boat, but Clem really keeps track of things and vouches for their whereabouts. I do feel that this is not a chance encounter as it's too far away in a very environmentally hostile area. I don't believe that a couple of airheads killed them for bunkum. Due to the heat and location, I just can't place any stock in that theory."

"Then, Jake, there is you. You know your way around the ranch and have had the most to gain by it. You're the ranch manager now, right? You don't have a past either. We can trace back only seven years. So, no offense, but you're number one on my list."

"Sheriff I appreciate your candor and sharing it with me. Don't spend too much time investigating me as I didn't do it."

CHAPTER 19

ONCE THE ROUND UP DATES WERE SET, CLEM HAD HIS crew cleaning up and doing repair work to the corrals. This became a major task considering not much had been done for a long time. Cowboys were sent out by Clem and were reporting back on the locations of stock and their condition. Milt Powers had run his bulls year round with the cows, so calves were being dropped all year long. Since the help he had employed were negligent, his stock losses ran higher than normal. Jake and Clem planned to change this practice. Therefore, they wanted to reduce the herd size by 75 per cent and sell off all the bulls. Several days before the round up any stock that came up to the ranch would be rounded up and kept in the repaired holding pastures and fed hay.

A local pilot named Fred Gill was employed to fly his hang glider over the entire area spotting groups of stock and their locations. On round up day he would fly again and radio his findings to Jake, who would then radio or cell phone the stocks location to whoever was the closest.

To everyone's amazement and pleasure, Jake's father, Jeff French, showed up and was a far cry from his normal, grumpy self. He likely realized his company would need to be turned over to the board and he should retire while he had some semblance of health left. Since Jake had found so much happiness of being of all things a cowboy, maybe ranch life would suit him too.

The next couple of days passed in a very casual manner. Joan showed Jeff around the ranch and took him on a couple of drives showing him the locale, countryside and the western way of life. She even got him some jeans, boots and shirts at the local western store. Jake noticed right away that his Dad seemed invigorated.

Jeff had now looked at the books and confided to Jake, "This is the slipperiest sided bunch of book keeping that I have ever seen. And I will say, as my son, I am very proud of what you have found. Tell you what. Let's consolidate most of this stuff and get it to make more sense. We won't make as much for a while, but we will get a better feel for where we are at, not looking for high yields or gains at this time. I'll only need to spend a few days on doing this. I love this life style. Join me on the patio, Jake, for a beer."

Tom and Bob, with their families, arrived on the Wednesday before the round up. The Powers boys and their families strolled around the Lazy 6 taking it all in. They, fortunately, had the good sense to tone down their dude appearance. Jake and Sylvia took them to the local title company office where all the papers were signed, transferring the ownership of the Lazy 6 ranch property to Sylvia. The Powers' boys were then paid with a money transfer directly into their accounts.

Round up Saturday was nearly upon them. Tom and Bob and their families were engaged in throwing unnecessary items out and packing up the house. They had scheduled movers to come out the following Wednesday and to have all wanted items hauled home.

Cassie and Jake were back at the trailer mansion, as Cassie called it. Jeff was at Joan's in the spacious spare bedroom. He called the office every day but spent less time now on his calls. He then spent a couple of hours doing ranch related bookkeeping and financial things. Then he would explore the ranch.

This pleased Jake to no end as it created more time to do what he wanted - cowboying. He compared notes with his father daily and enjoyed this one-on-one interaction with his dad. He hadn't spent this much time with his dad in years.

Jeff was quite enchanted with the nearly floor-to-ceiling windows throughout the house. He stared out at the unbelievable expansive views of far distant purple shrouded mountains, sunlight changing the colors on them frequently. It was apparent he was becoming a changed man, with energy levels rising. He wandered around the ranch talking to everybody, sitting on the back patio with Joan after supper, watching the sunset and evening closing in. Enjoying a beer or cocktail became an especially captivating experience. Jake knew his dad planned to leave shortly after the round up, but now began to wonder.

CHAPTER 20

CLEM GOODMAN WAS A GUY THAT LIKED TO ORGANIZE things, lining up this person or another for this job or that job. He always planned details into things. So with the upcoming round up, he was expecting about thirty riders of varying skills. He then would break them down into groups of six or so, mixing experience and ranch layout knowledge. Then he would add a few cowboys and few novice riders into the three groups that would then take stock trailers hauling their horses to far distant locations, cutting the actual ride time in half.

The other groups would then ride in specific locations that were closer to the corrals. The three main long distance riders were led by Ol' Wild Bill, Bob Bissell and Cassie. Clay Robertson and another rider from a nearby ranch, and who had been on numerous previous Lazy 6 round ups, took the two mid distant groups out. The rest of the groups were filled by less experienced riders and some that weren't up to long rides, but were still led by experienced cowboys.

Jake's father and two other stoved-up old timers would be the gate men. Jake questioned their experience and physical ability.

"What can be so hard about that?" Clem expressed. "All they got to do is slam the damn gate closed after whatever the group or riders bring in."

Jeff was introduced to his fellow gate men on the day before. They found they all had a lot in common. One was a banker, the other was a real estate man, both of whom had always cowboyed on the side. They said they always came on the day before to make sure all the gates would swing and latch closed. They set about checking everything, oiling the gates and clearing dirt and brush from the gates.

Jeff thought, "Maybe there is something more to this than meets the eye." Then his fellow gate men revealed to him that any round up that Clem planned always had exceptional food. So why not show up early to enjoy it?

As it was, Clem had lined up two cowboy chuck wagons and cooks to furnish genuine chuck wagon cooking to prepare over the next three days. They belonged to a chuck wagon group that participated all over the Southwest and other places in competition. All the cooking was done over open fires and Dutch ovens. A lot of people came just for the experience of genuine chuck wagon food. Sure enough, people began arriving early Friday afternoon. Both wagons had arrived the night before. The cooks had dug some large holes in the ground that they filled with mesquite and set on fire. Several smaller holes were dug for Dutch oven cooking. By Friday evening, barbecued beef was ready and the Dutch ovens yielded savory biscuits, beans and other sides.

CHAPTER 21

THE DAY BEFORE THE ROUND UP ALL SORTS OF PEOPLE HAD begun showing up at the Powers Lazy 6 Ranch. They camped in trailers, pick up campers, horse trailers with living quarters, tents and some with just spread air mattresses and blankets on the ground. The chuck wagons began serving all sorts of just that – round up food. Everyone was in high spirits. Many of the cowboys and girls practiced on roping on just about anything or anyone. Clem had felt he would need about thirty riders to gather all the stock in the morning, but he soon discovered he had about fifty. One of Clem's and Jake's innovations was two way radios for all the C-Bar Ranch hands. In addition, the hang glider would be furnished a radio. Clem had set up a large tent as an office. The riders were checked in by Joan, Cassie and Clem's wife and were told who they would ride with and where to meet up.

The remainder of the day was spent socializing and consuming chuck wagon barbecue. Some singing around the campfire took up the night. The principles in this round up turned in early as morning would be soon at hand.

A sunrise filled with gold, amber and yellow colors filled the morning sky. The clinking of kitchen activity gave sign to early morning life – Breakfast was on. Late arrivals for the round up had pulled in and soon breakfast was over. Horses were saddled up. Jake did a radio check and sent them all off to their appointed destinations.

Occasionally, the radio crackled with information on how various groups were progressing. By ten AM some of the cattle began coming in driven by riders who had started closer to the corrals. They came into the V shaped trap and then through the first holding pen gate. The gate men then slammed the gate closed. Jeff didn't think there was anything too hard about that.

At the first holding pen, Joan and Clem's wife recorded the number of stock, tag numbers, brands, of which some were missing, bulls and young calves that had not been worked yet. When this was done, the gate men opened another gate and drove the stock into a larger pen. This made Jeff think that this gate business was not too complicated.

Two more groups came in with a combined herd of something like twenty five head. When they were ready to move this bunch of cattle into a larger pen, the first group of cattle suddenly decided they wanted to come back to the smaller pen; more effort on the part of the gate men. Jeff was beginning to think this was more physical than what he thought.

Now the long riders were coming in. The process was the same, just taking more time. Jake then told the corral crew that all the riders were in and they would break for lunch and in the afternoon, they would weigh and ship stock for the cattle buyer and that tomorrow, Sunday, they would "work" the calves.

Jake ended up manning the radio on the ground and keeping track of where the riders were and where the airplane was.

Jake's father, along with the two other stoved-up former cowboys, manned the gates. Joan tallied the stock brought in, checked their brands, determined how many bulls were in the group and noted any ear tag numbers. Then the gate men drove them into a holding pasture.

Jeff thought, "There's definitely more to this then what it sounds like."

The Powers boys were awestruck when all these people with horses began showing up. They confided in Clem, "Do we have to pay all these people?"

Clem with a twinkle in his eye said, "No, just feed them and show up for their roundups. Neighbors help neighbors. It's been that way before I was born."

From the onset, Clem urged everyone to work the cattle slow and easy; none of this whooping and hollering seen on TV. So it wasn't a surprise when at one in the afternoon, all the riders were in and it was chuck wagon fare again. Jeff was clearly having the time of his life. And Jake and Joan had to slow him down to keep him from overdoing it.

"Wait till I get these photographer's pictures and send them to the crew at the office. They will all want to be out here." Jeff was elated.

By early afternoon, Nate Bloom had arrived with several semitrailers to haul his cattle away. They had agreed to use the scales Milt Powers had as they had recently been cleaned, worked on and certified by the weights and measurement inspector. The only disappointment came when it became apparent that only 331 cattle were actually rounded up. With cows dropping calves all year, this number should have been over 400. Clem and Jake knew, however, that Milt and his two cowboys didn't spend much time pasture checking stock, but the number missing still seemed high.

Sorting began after lunch. Ten to fifteen head of cattle were cut into a pen and slowly driven, single file, where Clem would call out whether to ship or save. The ship stock went right onto the scales where their weight and number was recorded. The saved cattle went into a holding pen to be weighed later. The gate men had to flip the sorting gate back and forth which exhausted Jeff.

Joan took it upon herself to drive him home, overriding his objections. He ultimately slept the afternoon, the evening and night away.

The cattle had been sorted and weighed and then loaded up into Nate Bloom's cattle trucks. Tom and Bob were pleased to get a big check.

Clem then weighed his thirty-eight head of now C-Bar stock. These consisted mostly of heifers, a few cows, three pregnant cows that Nate didn't want to fool with and two crippled up cows he didn't want either. Of these two cows, Clem planned to sell one to the local butcher shop, the other to supply meat for the ranch.

Sunday, they branded, gave shots and castrated the calves that were too small for Nate to take. The chuck wagon crew served a lunch and then cleaned up and loaded up. Everyone had a truly great time and even Sheriff Rogers had shown up and helped wrestle calves. Tom and Bob felt that this was the end of a unique experience and it would be something they would greatly miss.

Cassie told them, however, "Roundups come twice a year and I'll make sure you get an invitation."

CHAPTER 22

A FEW DAYS HAD PASSED AND EVERYONE SEEMINGLY got back to normal. Cassie and Jake were now contemplating moving into the Powers house. They began cleaning the house up some more and decided to have a local painter paint the entire inside of the house. They realized that this was a house of unique design. It was not based on the southwestern design, but based on a northern ranch house. The Powers apparently spent more money on the house than anything else on the ranch.

On the outside the walls were of river rock and pine logs. Large trees shaded the house on all sides but were not planted too densely as to detract the spacious views from the house. The front porch and back patio were well shaded inviting one to sit and relax.

Inside, the spacious and carefully thought out kitchen was easily accessible to the patio. It opened to a dining area and spacious living room complete with a massive river rock fireplace. Windows and patio doors with spectacular views were skillfully placed. A large office was squirreled away off to one side and provided a very private and secluded place to work. It also had beautiful large windows showing the beauty of the outside area.

CHAPTER 23

J EFF, ONE DAY SAID TO HIS SON, "JAKE, WHAT'S WITH THE Mexican restaurant you are always talking about?"

"You mean the Show Me Later Bar and Grill?"

"Yeah, the one where you say you do all your serious drinking and thinking. Let's go over there."

"I can't right now dad. Got a few things on my plate and I am pretty tied up. Tell you what. Turn on your charm and I bet you can get Joan and Cassie to take you over there for lunch today."

It took no effort to get the girls to take Jeff to the Show Me Later. They went in Cassie's new pickup. Jeff remarked, "I don't understand that boy of mine. He could have a truck like this with all the comforts, but he drives that old truck of his like it's the best thing that ever happened to him. I don't understand. Do you, Cassie?"

"No Jeff," she replied. "And I haven't known him for very long. He can drive this truck any time he wants, but almost never does. He seems a very happy person, riding horses, chasing cows, being outside, reclining on our patio with a mesquite fire in the fire pit. You know, about the same thing goes for me, too."

Jeff was impressed with the Show Me Later. "Seems they spent a lot of money making this a special place, but I wonder why as it's out here in the middle of nowhere."

Joan could only say, "I don't know either, but they do get pretty busy on weekends."

They were seated by Mode, a slender young girl who took over running the restaurant any time the owner was gone on his many trips. She took their orders and served their drinks; Beer for Jeff and Cassie, a large Margarita for Joan. A man served them with chips and salsa and when he departed, Joan whispered to Cassie, "That's him!"

"That's who?" Cassie asked.

'The ATV driver who took us out," Joan answered. Joan began to get very agitated as it brought up recent memories, so Jeff got her started on her margarita. When Mode brought their lunches, Jeff asked her who was the man that brought the chips and salsa.

Mode said. "That is Manuel Ortez, the restaurant owner. He likes to help out and ensure prompt service." He was out for a bit but came back to help.

"That's great." Jeff commented.

After lunch and back at the truck, Joan said, "That was him alright. What's going on anyway?"

Back at the ranch, upon telling Jake, he only said, "The Sheriff will really enjoy this news."

CHAPTER 24

THE SHERIFF AND DEPUTY GREG BURGER IMMEDIATELY came out to the Show Me Later and picked up Manuel telling him they had some questions they wanted to ask him and that it would be best to go down to the Sheriff's office where they wouldn't have any interruptions. Manuel seemed undisturbed by this and they all made light conversation.

They sat in a small interview room where Sheriff Rogers explained that this was about an ATV trip where Manuel had taken five people out into the desert.

"What's with this ATV stuff, Manuel?"

"A friend of mine takes ATV tours out from his place in Sedona. Sometimes he runs short of drivers and I fill in."

"Does this happen very often?"

"Yeah, I go up there four or five times a week. It pays in tips real good."

"You took a group out from the Lazy Six Ranch. Wasn't that a little unusual?"

"No, I do that more often than you think. I do like doing custom trips."

"Did your boss set this Lazy Six trip up?"

Manuel answered, "No I got a letter from them that they wanted me to take them out for a trip."

"Mailed to you?"

"No, hand delivered to my restaurant. It was on my desk."

"Do you still have the letter?"

"No, I was done with it and threw it away."

"What did it say and who was it from?"

"It said to pick up four people at the Lazy Six ranch and take them to a campsite shown on a very descriptive map. This was to be a special treat for them, so I was not to talk to anyone about this. It also included $300 in cash."

Intrigued the Sheriff asked, "How did the letter sender know you would show up and didn't this whole thing seem a little strange?"

"Well, sort of. But the $300 was not. I didn't really have a way to answer as I didn't know where the letter came from. So I borrowed an ATV from my boss in Sedona and hauled it to my restaurant on Thursday night. On Friday,

I drove it to the Lazy Six, only now a young girl showed up also. She said she was a photographer, but she really didn't take very many pictures and seemed to have been invited by Mildred."

"Manuel, did you know any of these five people you took out."

"No."

"What about anyone at the Lazy Six or C-Bar Ranch. Do you know any of them?"

"I really don't think so, but my sister, who I don't see very often, works for the girl in the big white house out there. This girl is sort of a strange girl and a real loner."

"What is your sister's name?"

"Juanita."

Sheriff Rogers then went over the whole scene again and somehow was convinced Manuel had told him all that he knew. A Deputy was dispatched to take him back to his restaurant. A second Deputy was sent to pick up Juanita before Manuel could contact her if he was so inclined.

Juanita accompanied the Deputy only inquiring as to what this was all about. He replied he didn't know and was just following orders. The Sheriff realized he hadn't learned very much new information. But he had at least some answers to these murders. Unfortunately, Juanita could only add very little to this scene. She and her brother were not very close and rarely had any contact. She had only talked to him maybe six months ago. She didn't think Sylvia or any of the ranch people even knew who he was.

Sylvia was out of town at this time and she really didn't know where she was. Juanita did say that the first she heard anything about the lost hikers was on Saturday night long past their failed return home, when one of the Lazy Six cowboys called Sylvia.

Sylvia, upon her return home, did call the Sheriff confirming no previous knowledge of this planned hike and camping trip. She also confirmed that the first she learned of any of this was when one of the two Lazy Six cowboys called to say the Powers were gone and nowhere to be seen. And that Milt had casually mentioned to one of the cowboys that they should be back by Saturday morning.

Again, she confirmed about being called late Saturday night and that this was the first she heard anything about this camping trip.

Now Sheriff Rogers wanted to question the two Lazy 6 Cowboys as they apparently had some previous awareness of this camping trip. They were not hard to find as they were still in the County jail awaiting trial for cattle rustling. One said he didn't know anything about any of this. The other said he had talked with Milt casually about the trip the night before and confirmed that they expected to be back by Saturday morning.

Because of the high heat, he became concerned when they didn't show up at sundown. The only person he thought to call was Sylvia. She told him to search their ranch and she'd have the C-Bar cowboys out looking on the ranch at dawn.

Sheriff Rogers and his two deputies digested this information over the next few months. They knew who had taken them to the wrong starting point. The map would have been a key to finding out the error of the drop off point. That Juanita and Manuel were brother and sister opens the question of their involvement. Neither had an alibi for their whereabouts at the time of the murders, but for that matter the two Lazy Six cowboys didn't either. Rogers felt that the mysterious Lois held the answers and surely she would show up sooner or later.

CHAPTER 25

J EFF FRENCH HAD STAYED ON AT JOAN'S HOUSE AND HAD decided shortly after Thanksgiving he was going to cash in his chips and retire. The investment company was incorporated and all he had to do was resign as Board Chairman and clean out his office. He flew to Chicago and did just that. More decisions had to be made. What about his house on the lake and the three people who had worked for his family for years?

He took a bold step and asked Joan to join him in Chicago until Christmas. She arrived in his usual chartered private Lear jet. For the next few days he squired her around to the better restaurants and social events.

Jeff, after a few days, asked Joan about her impressions of the big city life.

"Jeff, this is really an experience and you've made this trip delightful and memorable, but for me this is not my lifestyle. I don't need a chauffeur, a maid or a housekeeper. If you want, come back to the ranch and we can pick up where we left off."

Jeff lapsed into deep thought. "Thank you, Joan, for being so honest." He said. "It's about what I thought you would say. I don't think I want to do this big city thing any more. I think, after the First of the year, I'll sell this house. Have an estate sale on the furnishings, sell the cars and pension my three remaining employees. Let's photograph everything and see if the kids want anything. It's a little cold up here right now and the snow is piling up. I sure miss a fire in the fire pit and a glass of wine in the patio after a full day of varied work and thinking what we might do the next day."

The selling of the house and cars was finished in March as was the estate sale. The three employees were retired and pensioned. Some furniture and boxes of personal items were hauled away by the movers to the ranch and unloaded at Jake and Cassie's house. About this time Clay Robertson had taken up with a local girl and they moved into the trailer mansion. Bob Bissell had a truck accident that left him pretty crippled up and forced him to retire. Clem kept him on with a pension deal set up with Jeff and had him working around the barns and corrals, keeping everything up in tiptop shape. Clem then suggested hiring Clay's girlfriend,

Becky, to replace Bob. Becky came from a local ranching family and was a very good roper. She wanted to follow the cowboy ways. When Clem suggested that they hire Becky, Jake suggested that they draw straws on this one too.

LOIS IS FOUND

CHAPTER 26

THAT SUMMER LAW ENFORCEMENT CAUGHT UP WITH THE mysterious Louisa Handback. She was picked up in Cleveland, Ohio while taking part in trying to rob a bank with two accomplices. Sheriff Rogers decided to interview her in Cleveland taking with him Deputy Greg Burger.

In Cleveland, they met with the local detectives and after some small talk, Lois was brought to an interview room equipped with video and recording devices. They read her rights to her to which afterwards she said to continue as she was "cooked" anyway.

"How did you get involved with this so called camping trip?" Rogers asked.

She replied, "I was living in Wilcox. I was working as a waitress at a local restaurant. One day a busboy handed me

an envelope with my name on it. I opened it later that night. The letter said that the writer wanted me to go on an overnight hike and camping trip. I was to pose as a photographer and explain why I showed up unexpectedly at the last minute. I was to say that I had been invited by Mildred Powers."

"Secondly, I was to make sure the two men separated from the women. I was then to convince the women to return to well No. 1."

"Third, I was to plant a tracking device on either one of the men or in one of their backpacks."

Sheriff Rogers then asked, "Why did you become a part of this rather bizarre scheme?"

She replied, "In that envelope was $2,000."

"What then?"

"The letter also said if I accomplished those three things, to get out of town as fast as I could. Upon returning to my apartment, I was to look under my door and there was to be another envelope containing an additional $2,000. So I did. And there was the money under my door. But at this time I realized that this was a wrong thing to do. I got really scared. I knew Mildred had died and somehow it was likely the two men had passed also."

"Who was behind this whole event?" Rogers asked.

"I really don't know," she replied.

"Mildred, I suppose. But from the onset, she was pretty sick and didn't seem to be very aware of things."

Rogers and Burger compared notes after the interview and agreed there had to be another person involved. Most likely it was Manuel or one of the two Lazy 6 cowboys.

CHAPTER 27

TWO YEARS HAD PASSED SINCE THEY CAUGHT LOIS. LOUISA had been sentenced and jailed in Cleveland for attempted bank robbery. The two former Lazy 6 cowboys had also been sentenced and jailed for cattle rustling. Over the last couple of years; however, the three had been interviewed on several occasions as was Manuel and Juanita. Nothing new came forth, however.

Clay Robertson and Becky had gotten married and had a son. The twenty four foot travel trailer frequently referred to as "the mansion" had been hauled away and replaced by a much larger single wide trailer in which Clay and Becky made their home.

Jake fussed over the whole project, particularly the covered patio and tree placement. Clay kidded him about his concern. Jake simply stared at him and said, "I'll trade you."

It wasn't a surprise when a year before Jake's father married Joan. They had become a very compatible couple. He enjoyed doing the ranch books and modest investing in the stock market; particularly his pleasure came walking around the ranch and talking to everyone, especially Bob Bissell. Joan was an eager travel partner on the many short trips they took by car.

The bizarre management system continued to flourish. Although his dad had taken over the books, Jake still signed all the checks. Jake and Clem conferred on everything. Clem basically continued to run the ranch. Jake rode most of the time now doing cowboy stuff and ranch maintenance. They sponsored photography clinics several times a year, chuck wagon contests were held at the twice annual round ups, several horsemanship clinics were held with noted clinicians and with obstacle course challenges.

By this time Cassie now began peppering Jake with hints about getting married.

CHAPTER 28

THAT SAME YEAR AT THE ANNUAL FALL ROUNDUP A LARGE number of people showed up as usual on Friday. Kids were playing everywhere. Some were down in a wash pretending to be outlaws robbing a stagecoach. The monsoon season rains had washed the dirt and rocks from the creek bed creating a ledge about six feet high from which the outlaw playing kids were attacking a pretend stagecoach.

A chunk of the ledge broke away exposing a side of the ledge. One of the boys saw something wrapped in plastic. They dug it out of the side of the ledge. One of the ten year old boys remarked that it looked like a gun. They wanted to unwrap it to make sure.

"No," one of the boys said, "It might be loaded and I think that we should get it to my dad."

At that they all trooped over to the boy's dad who was talking to Jake. Jake knew right away what they had found.

"Let's not unwrap it and you boys don't go back there until the Sheriff arrives. Then you can go back there with the Sheriff and show him where you found this gun."

Upon calling Sheriff Rodgers, he told Jake to put it in a plastic bag just as it had been found. And keep everyone away from the site where it had been found. Jake could sense the excitement in the Sheriff's voice and thought to himself, "This could be it."

Rogers, along with Deputies Greg Burger and Tom Hickman arrived quickly. The three patrol cars drew quite a crowd. Rogers recruited Jake, Clay, Ol' Wild Bill and Jeff French to keep the crowd away from the discovery site.

The deputies photographed everything in sight noting Sylvia's white house was seen in the background. Wayne asked if Sylvia was home.

Jake said he didn't really think so, but didn't know for sure.

The Sheriff and the Deputies left saying they would be in touch.

On Monday the Sheriff called Jake and told him that the gun had belonged to Sylvia's father. Further, the test bullets fired from it matched those that had killed Carson Smith and Milt Powers.

Jake drove over to Sylvia's house to see if she or Juanita were there. No one answered the door which he found to be unlocked. He thought he would check the garage and see what cars were gone. There he found Juanita's and Sylvia's cars indeed gone. Glancing around he noticed bicycles and what appeared to be a couple of motor cycles covered with canvass. Peaking under the canvass he found a standard Kawasaki dirt bike and an electric dirt bike.

He called the Sheriff's office explaining what he had found and when Sylvia or Juanita had returned he would call.

On Wednesday, Sylvia returned and Jake somehow felt for whatever reason she was going to leave again soon, so he drove over to her house. He rang the bell and she came to the door looking somewhat distraught. He simply said, "Hello, I was hoping to catch you home."

"Well, come on in," she said. "You know, don't you?" She added.

"He stated, "Know what?"

She answered and then completely broke down crying uncontrollably then became hysterical.

Jake did get a call off to Rogers. Sylvia through all of this said, "I knew I'd get caught sooner or later and I was scared all the time. All of this consumed my life and made a wreck out of me. I couldn't function. I made so many mistakes and you are one of them, Jake. I'm so sorry I let you slip through my fingers."

Jake said, "Let's go to the kitchen and make some coffee. It might make talking to the Sheriff easier."

Rogers showed up about the time the coffee was ready. They sat in the living room. Rogers read Sylvia her rights and said he would record the conversation.

She told them, "Milt Powers had it in for Mildred and they hadn't gotten along for years. He had felt she spent way too much money on the house and other things she liked. He spent a lot of time hitting on me and chasing after me. In part that's why I was gone a lot. Carson Smith was collateral damage. I knew he was stealing from me. I tried to fire him, but everything was either in his name or on a lesser scale, my father's. Mildred came up with this bizarre plan as she felt her husband was trying to kill her, but she didn't know how. I wrote those letters and made the map. I also contacted Manuel through Juanita. Juanita delivered the letters and put the money underneath Lois' door. Juanita basically arranged the ATV trip with Manuel and, really, he was innocent as he didn't know about the well switch."

"Juanita came up with Lois and Mildred made arrangements with her about this trip. It was easy to track the two men on my battery operated dirt bike. I snuck up on them, shot them and retrieved the tracking device. I dug a hole with a posthole digger one night out by that dry wash. Then I buried the gun thinking it would never be found."

"Jake, if you would, call a lawyer for me. I can afford a good one. I really don't want to be bailed out either, too many crazy people around."

"You are right about a road to the cabin, but it washed out years ago. My mother and dad didn't get along very well and my dad took me to the cabin by horseback many times when I was little, just to get away from mom. Later we'd go by dirt bike when I was big enough to ride one."

"Why dad built the cabin, I never knew. After he passed away, I spent even more time back there. I know my way around there better than anybody. Good-bye, Jake. Sorry I never really got to know you. Marry that girl you got, Jake. She's a prize. Have a long life together."

CHAPTER 29

U LTIMATELY, SYLVIA IN A SOMEWHAT DRAWN OUT TRIAL got a life sentence with a chance of parole in twenty. Juanita was sentenced to six years for conspiracy and aiding to commit a murder.

Cassie and Jake got married that year. He drove his old truck. She drove the new one. The same bizarre management system continued except now they spent one afternoon a month in a board meeting. On one occasion Clem brought up what to do about Sylvia's house as it was not used or even a practical, marketable item.

Jake suggested selling everything in it and tearing it down. Clay thought that was a great idea as he never liked the monstrosity in the first place.

Bob Bissell said, "What happens if she ever gets out?"

Clay said, "With this savings program which Jeff has for all of us, she can build a smaller, much more practical one."

Clem said, "Do we need to draw straws on this?"

Jake said, "No, it's a done deal."

ABOUT THE AUTHOR

R ON MCCOY, HAS BEEN WRITING AND WORKING WITH horses and cattle for over sixty years. He has participated in numerous roundups in Texas and Arizona. Trail riding has always been his favorite pastime along with writing. Illinois, Arkansas, Texas, Colorado, Kansas, Ohio, Indiana, Tennessee, Kentucky, and Arizona are some of the many places he's called home at one time or another.

Ron has served as Director and Board Chairman of The Indiana Trail Riders Association for several years. He has worked on ranches and boarding stables in his retirement years.

This is Ron's second book. His first book *Campfire Tales and Other Adventures* is a collection of some sixty humorous stories. All events actually happened. Ron has always felt that life is an adventure. "But you must seek it out yourself. No one will hand it to you on a silver platter."